JUST A SIMPLE COUNTRY BOY

A Novel

JAMES H. TAIT

authorHOUSE®

AuthorHouse™
1663 Liberty Drive
Bloomington, IN 47403
www.authorhouse.com
Phone: 833-262-8899

Published by AuthorHouse 10/26/2021

ISBN: 978-1-6655-3723-0 (sc)
ISBN: 978-1-6655-3721-6 (hc)
ISBN: 978-1-6655-3722-3 (e)

Library of Congress Control Number: 2021918134

Print information available on the last page.

Any people depicted in stock imagery provided by Getty Images are models, and such images are being used for illustrative purposes only. Certain stock imagery © Getty Images.

This book is printed on acid-free paper.

FOREWORD

This is a fictional crime story interwoven with actual historical facts. Most of the named places gives their real locations and origins. All characters are figments of my imagination except for one prominent industrialist and entrepreneur who lived in Newcastle upon Tyne and became a baronet.His surname and that of his fictitious great niece has been changed.His country mansion in Northumberland has been fictitiously renamed but still exists as a museum under the ownership of the National Trust.All criminal activity that took place at this location as recorded in this novel is imaginary.

CHAPTER 1. HOW IT ALL BEGAN

Tom Stearsby sat on the edge of his prison cot with his fingers clasped loosely together between his denimed knees, staring at the narrow shaft of sunlight that had slipped through the bars of the high window of his cell and formed a yellow pool on the floor on the stone floor. It reminded him of the day he had sat beside Mary's bed in the hospital Intensive Care unit and watched her life slowly ebb away.The rays of the setting sun at the end of a long afternoon had pierced the gloom of curtained room through a half-opened window; Tom had stared at a finger of light as it crept down the wall to rest on Mary's waxen brow. Hope leapt into his heart as he imagined the golden shaft to be a sign of benediction. In that moment he prayed for its warmth and power to penetrate his wife's body and heal her wounds, but the fantasy dissolved with the fading of the beam, leaving only the deadly chill of despair to freeze his mind and spirit.

Six feet to his right Frankie Stevens was slouched against the steel corner post of his bunk picking at his teeth with a grimy fingernail.He was waiting for morning mess call which was late in coming.He was not in any great hurry to get to the lumpy porridge,cold dried egg and greasy streaky bacon that made up breakfast but he was anxious to escape from the sullen,silent presence of his cell mate.The guy gave him the creeps.Ever since the Parole Board had turned his plea for an early release he had been deaf and mute.What did he expect?You cannot kill a man in cold blood and hope to be freed for good behaviour after just two years!He was lucky to get the sentence he did.He should have been given Life! Look at himself. Fifteen years for a shooting accident.It was not his fault that the kid wanted to be a hero.He shouldn't have tried to wrestle him for the gun. It wasn't his money,was it?He was lucky that the bullet only went into his shoulder instead of his head.Fifteen years?You can't call that justice.OK,so it was not his first armed robbery but he had not shot any one before.He should have been the one up for parole. The police had recovered most of the money,hadn't they?

Frankie shot a furtive glance at the crouching figure.He looked so pathetic that you could not imagine him having the guts to kill anyone.But then,who can tell?He had once shared a cell with Charlie Warren,who was a pintsized weedy runt who had raped and strangled four women.He had looked like a man who could not hurt a fly.Except for his eyes!When Charlie focussed them on you through his horn-rimmed glasses you felt like a rabbit hypnotised by a snake.A shiver ran down Frankie's spine.Even though it was two years since Charlie was hanged he could still feel the cold sweat break out on his back whenever he thought of those cold emotionless eyes It was like looking into a dark pit where monsters lurked.

Frankie stared again at his cell mate who had not moved from his position.This guy was deep,alright.He did not scare you like Charlie did but the silent types were always the worst.You could never fathom what was going on his head.Talking to him was like trying to talk to one of those waxwork figures in Madame Tussauds.You never got an answer.Frankie shook a puzzled head.He had spent most of his life in prison and associated with criminal gangs when he was on the outside but he had never met a guy who acted like Stearsby did.When he was not staring at the high window above the landing he had his head in a book. A crime thriller by Mickey Spillane might be ok if you could follow the plot and even a men's magazine like Playboy,though that could get you all fidgety in a joint like this,but natural life stories about animals? Give me a break! They are only useful when they are dead.He enjoyed a tasty steak sirloin and even pork ribs,but caring for cows,sheep and pigs and mucking out while they were alive was a job for oddballs.

Stevens had a sudden thought that made him straighten up from his slouched position.Hey,hang on a minute! Perhaps this guy is not so queer after all!Suppose he has been thinking about breaking out? Is that why he keeps looking up at that window?Nuts!You would have to be a bird to get out that way!But suppose he could escape somehow?He would be on the run and have to keep out of sight, wouldn't he?Frankie saw his cellmate in a new light. Well, I'm damned! He stared at Stearsby's hunched back.So that's it!No wonder he did not have time for small talk.He was too preoccupied working out an escape plan and how he would survive once he was outside.It occurred to Frankie that it would pay him to be more friendly with his cellmate. If he was planning a prison break he may be persuaded that two had a better chance than one on his own.He should have ignored Stearsby's silences and tried to build up a friendship. He was contemplating how to breach the defences of his tight-lipped companion when shrill whistles cut into his thoughts. The warders' blasts were followed by the loud clanging of the cell doors along the landing as they were simultaneously slid open.

CHAPTER 2. INCARCERATION

Down below in the huge mess hall, Tom lined up with the other prisoners and collected his breakfast, not bothering to look at what was spooned on to his plate. He queued up again to fill up his tin mug from one of the large tea urns and took his tray to an empty table. Around him the babble of raucous male voices and the clatter of plates and utensils swirled and eddied but he was barely conscious of the din. His mind floated away as he chewed mechanically on the prison diet and suddenly he was in the hills above Cornchester ankle deep in purple heather and wild gorse. The sun was hot on his head and there was a murmuring of bees and the cracking of bursting gorse pods in his ears as he watched two brown linnets wheel and dart in flight. He was on the edge of the pine coppice, home for red squirrels and roedeer, crossbills and tawny owls. Beside him his tousled eared terrier Benjie stood expectantly, sniffing the breeze while waiting for his master to move on. But Tom was in no hurry. This was his place. Here he was free.Only here could he fill his lungs with the clean pure air that helped to refresh his spirit.Only here could he feel some lifting of the depression that had overwhelmed him since Mary's death.

"Shove over, mate." The growl was accompanied by a sharp dig in the ribs that brought Tom back into reality.He looked into the glowering face of a fellow convict.

"Sorry, chum," he apologised, shifting his body to make room at the end of the bench. He wanted no trouble.

"I was just going, anyway."The man pointed at the half -eaten rasher of streaky bacon that remained on Tom's plate

''I will have that if you do not want it.What's the matter,mate? Are you a fussy eater or do you have your mind on a bit of skirt outside?"

Tom made no reply as the fatty piece of cold bacon was scooped from his plate.He stood up and stepped backwards free of the bench. Looking around at all the blue garbed figures hunched over their food and the silent uniformed guards pacing slowly up and down between the rows of benches he clenched his fists.

"God!How I hate this place!"

CHAPTER 3. HORROR

Back in his cell, and with his cellmate still in the mess hall,Tom lay on his bunk and let his mind drift away again. He had been up in the top field that morning searching for the den of a raiding fox when he heard the gunshots.Three quickly in succession, the sounds resonating in the air. At first he thought that it was Johnson, his neighbouring farmer,using his shotgun to kill a rabbit or a pigeon,but then he realised that the sound of the shots had not come from the farm but from the direction of the village. Moreover, the sharp cracks sounded more like rifle or pistol fire than shotgun blasts.That thought brought instant alarm. Why would anyone be firing guns in the village?

Tom knew that Mary had planned to take the short walk to Janet's,the baby wear shop next to the Post Office with the intention of buying more clothing for the expected child.He became concerned by the thought that she may have been caught up in a serious incident but he quickly reassured himself. Nonsense! Nothing ever happened in the village.It was too small a backwater to attract any criminal element.Nevertheless, he whistled to his terrier and strode off at a quick pace towards his cottage. He would check to see if Mary was home before going to the village to find out what had caused the shots.The sound of an ambulance bell set him into a trot.He arrived at the door of Wisteria Cottage in a breathless state of anxiety. He lifted the latch and pushed the door wide open.Benjie bounded past him, tail wagging furiously.

"Mary! Mary! Are you here?"

No answer.Tom went into the kitchen,then called upstairs.

"Mary,are you there?"

Silence.Tom opened the back door and looked into the garden.There was washing drying on the clothesline but no Mary.He left Benjie to guard the premises and broke into a run towards the village.

CHAPTER 4. DISBELIEF

As Tom turned into the cobbled mainstreet of Cornchester he could see the small parade of shops ahead. A crowd gathered outside the post office where a police car and an ambulance were parked side by side. What was going on? He reached the back of the crowd and found a gap between two inquisitive heads that gave him a view of the doorway. A uniformed constable stood guard, blocking the interior.

"What has happened?" Tom enquired of no-one in particular.A middle-aged man in front of him turned his head."There has been a raid. Two armed men tried to rob the post office. The Postmaster tried to stop them and was shot."

"Good God!" exclaimed Tom. "Is he dead?"

"Don't know" was the answer. "He is still inside, lying on the floor. Two ambulance men are with him. A passer-by was shot as well. A woman had just come out of Janet's and bumped into one of the robbers as they fled. She looked pregnant but one of them still shot her, the bastard!"

Tom stared unbelieving at his informant.

"What? What? Where is she?"

"She was carried into the ambulance. They say that she was hit in the stomach. There was blood all over her front."

Tom stood aghast. He turned to the emergency vehicle. The back door was wide open. He elbowed two onlookers aside and stumbled towards it. Two other ambulancemen were inside bending over a still form. An oxygen mask covered the victim's face but Tom knew instantly that it was Mary. "Excuse me," he blurted out. "I think that is my wife! Is she badly hurt?"

One of the attendants turned his head.

"Sorry, sir, but the lady has not yet been identified. If you think that she may be your wife you should speak to the police. Were you with the lady when she was shot?"

Tom gripped the ambulance door and took a step up into the vehicle. He shook his head.

"No, but I am sure it is my wife. Please let me look."

The medic glanced at his colleague and hesitated before replying. Then he asked,

"Is your wife pregnant, sir?"

The young farmer felt himself tremble.

"Yes, she is. Eight months."

"Then, this may be your wife, sir. What is her name?"

"Mary, Mary Stearsby. Please let me see her!"

"All right, but just for a moment, just to confirm her identity. She is badly hurt and we need to get her to hospital. We are just waiting for the other victim to be brought out."

Tom's arm was held in a firm grip as he looked down on Mary's ashen face. Her eyes were closed. A blanket was drawn up to her neck covering her body. There was blood at the corner of her mouth.

"Oh, God!" Tom began to tremble more violently.

"Steady, sir steady."

The voice tried to calm him.

"It is definitely your wife, then?"

Tom nodded, almost too choked to speak.

"Yes, yes! Please help her!"

"We are doing all we can, Sir. We will get to the hospital as quickly as possible. Do you have a motor car?"

The question was answered with a shake of the head. Tom knew that his old truck would not keep up with ambulance.

"Right, the police will drive you to the hospital. Their car will escort us to clear any traffic."

There was a movement at the ambulance door. The two medics who had been inside the post office attending to the injured manager had stretchered his prone figure to the emergency vehicle. Tom stood aside as the stretcher was lifted and placed beside Mary. An accompanying police officer looked at him curiously.

"Who are you, sir?"

"He is the husband of the injured lady," replied the medic who had been holding Tom's arm. He has identified her. Can you give him a lift to the hospital?"

"Of course. We will drive ahead if you are ready to go?"

The medic nodded and closed the back of the ambulance as the officer took Tom to the escorting vehicle. He spoke to the driver.

"Let's go. And don't dilly dally. Use the siren."

CHAPTER 5. GRAPPLING WITH REALITY

The drive to the local hospital took less than twenty minutes with the ambulance following speedily behind, its bell clanging furiously. Tom sat in a daze in the rear seat of the police car staring blankly at the hedgerows as they flew by the window. He was jerked from his cataleptic state by the police sergeant's voice.

"I had better have your details, sir. The full names of you

and your wife, please, and your ages and address. Do you have any identification on you?"

Tom patted his trouser pockets.

"Sorry, no. I was working on my farm when I heard the gun shots and hurried straight to the village."

"Never mind, sir. We can check later. So, your full names, please."

"Tom Edward Stearsby. I am 25. I am a local farmer. My wife's name is Mary Ann. She is twenty two. We live at Wisteria Cottage, Bakers Lane, Cornchester."

Tom blinked a tear away as his eyes began to moisten. His voice began to break as he added,

"We are expecting our first child."

There was a moment of silence before the Sergeant quietly replied.

"We will be at the hospital in a few minutes. I have relayed ahead so doctors will be waiting to give your wife urgent attention. The postmaster too, of course."

The tarmaced drive of the hospital came into view. Tom glanced back to ensure that the ambulance was close behind as the police car drew up to the main entrance. As soon as both vehicles came to a stop he jumped out and ran round to the back door of the ambulance to assist the stretcher bearers carrying Mary and the postmaster. There was no need. A group of medical staff came forward and gathered around. The two stretchers were quickly transported into the hospital. Tom tried to get to Mary's side but he was ushered aside. He felt momentarily angered before realising that his presence was of no consequence since all the focus would be on the two gunshot victims. He was immensely grateful for that, but as he was directed into an empty waiting room and told to wait he was consumed by a dreadful feeling of isolation.

Tom stood staring blankly at the hospital grounds through a window for twenty minutes before the waiting room door opened and a brown suited registrar entered and introduced himself. He held a small board on which a blank medical questionnaire was pinned. He held out a neatly manicured hand and gave an apologetic smile.

"Sorry to keep you waiting, Sir. We had to get your wife into surgery. I am afraid that I need to ask you some questions about..........".

Tom interrupted.

"How is she? Please, how badly is she hurt? What about the baby?"

The registrar pointed to a green leather padded chair and indicated that Tom should sit down.

"I am sorry. I can only tell you that your wife suffered a serious gunshot wound to her stomach. She is being urgently prepared for investigative surgery. She is in the very capable hands of our senior surgeon. I am afraid that all you can do is sit and wait. You will be informed as soon as your wife comes out of theatre."

"But the baby? What about the baby?" Tom insisted.

The registrar held up a restraining hand.

"Ultrasound scans and other tests are being carried out right now.I cannot give you any information until those checks have been completed.Be assured that Mr Page will do everything possible to save your wife and child."

There was a vagueness about this reply that disturbed Tom but before he could question further the registrar held up the clipboard.

'"We need your wife's personal details,sir.Can I have her full name and date of birth, please, and her nationality and religion and the name of her GP?"

Tom answered all the questions until his interviewer seemed satisfied.

"Thank you, Mr. Stearsby.You can wait here or go home if you wish.I expect your wife will be in surgery for an hour or two, so you should try to get some rest. I have your home telephone number and I will arrange for someone to ring you as soon as your wife is out of surgery."

Tom shook his head.

"No, No. I want to stay here if that is OK?"

The registrar nodded.

"As you wish,Mr Stearsby.I know it is difficult but try not to worry.Your wife is in good hands."

As the registrar was exiting the room Tom suddenly remembered the Postmaster.

""The postmaster? Do you have an information about him?"

The registrar paused."Sorry. Only that he received chest and shoulder wounds.It is too early to say how serious they are but he is being attended to."

The door closed and Tom was left alone with his thoughts.They tumbled around in his mind like clothes spinning wildly in a washing machine.He felt completely disorientated,struggling in a morass of disbelief that refused to accept the horror of the events of the last few hours.None of this could be happening.

CHAPTER 6. DESPAIR

Three and a half increasingly anxious hours later the waiting room door opened.Tom stopped pacing and held his breath as a man dressed in green surgical garb entered. A green mask was draped loosely around his neck; a green skull cap was held in one hand.He looked gravely at Tom.

"I am Mr Page, the senior surgeon here. I presume you are Mr.Stearsby?"

He did not wait for answer.

"I have been attending to your wife.It is not good news I am afraid.She has been badly wounded.We have managed to stop the haemorrhaging for now and repair some of the damage but she is very poorly.She has been taken to the Intensive Care Unit where she will be closely monitored. You can go along to see her for a few moments but she is heavily sedated."

Tom felt himself trembling again. There was a lead weight in his chest. He stood silent with his eyes closed with a choking lump in his throat. Finally he was able to stumble out his question.

"And the baby?"

The surgeon sighed.

"I am afraid that we could not save the child. The bullet that struck your wife entered her uterus. His death would have been instantaneous. He would have felt nothing."

Tom stared at him.

"He? It was a boy?"

There was a nod.

"Yes. I am sorry. You would have had a son."

Tom felt faint. His legs turned suddenly to jelly. He dropped into the leather chair behind him. He heard the surgeon say,

"I will get someone to sit with you. Just stay where you are."

Tom struggled to regain his feet as the surgeon turned away.

"NO, no! I want to see my wife!"

The physician paused in his stride.

"Alright, Mr Stearsby."

He nodded to a waiting nurse.

"This nurse will take you to her,but please bear in mind that your wife's condition is very serious.The next twenty -four hours will be critical and she will remain under sedation.You can stay as long as you wish providing you keep your emotions under control and allow all the medical staff to perform their duties without interruption."

There was a softening of expression that took the harsh edge off the caveat. "Everything will be done to save your wife, Mr Stearsby.You may be assured of that."

The senior ward nurse led Tom across the corridor to the ITU. She pressed a bell to release the door lock and took the wet eyed young farmer to a small dimly lit room. Another nurse was making notes on a chart at the bottom of the bed where Mary was lying motionless beneath a white coverlet.She looked up at the two arrivals.

Tom was introduced.

"This is Mr Stearsby.He is going to sit with his wife."

The junior nurse smiled sympathetically.

'I will get a chair."

Tom nodded his thanks with eyes fixed on Mary's face. The dark lashes of her closed eyes contrasted with the pallor of her cheeks.With her hair brushed back from her forehead and spread luxuriantly on the pillows behind her she seemed in calm repose.There was no sign that she was not in a natural sleep except for the brightly lit monitor that bleeped steadily above her head.Tom tried not to look at the metal stand which held the drip feed bottle and the line which intravenously pumped drugs and nutrients into her body.They were part of the nightmare that he wanted to shut out from his mind.He pulled his chair closer to the bed and took hold of Mary's limp hand,praying that his touch would relay his love for her and bring her comfort.

He did not know how long he sat there,gazing at his wife's face,seeking some sign that she was holding her own.He stirred only when the nurse entered briefly to check the monitor and drip line before tiptoeing out again. He fell asleep for a short while in the early hours of the night and only a light touch on his shoulder startled him awake.A nurse was gazing down at him with a half-smile on her face.Tom struggled up from his slumped posture feeling guilty.He glanced at Mary but there was no change in the position of the still form in the bed.

"Sorry,Mr Stearsby would you mind waiting outside for a moment? A doctor wants to examine your wife."

Tom tried to clear his head."Oh,yes,sorry."

He saw the white coated male figure behind the nurse. He hesitated, searching for the right words.

"Is my wife....all right?"

"Her blood pressure has dropped a little.Don't worry.I will call you back in a little while."

Tom was gently ushered out of the room.The promised moment extended to an anxious half hour during which time he paced up and down impatiently as nursing staff came and went by with medical equipment. Finally the doctor appeared.

"I am sorry, Mr Stearsby. I am afraid that I will have to take your wife back into surgery. Why don't you go back home and get some rest?"

Tom shook his vehemently.

"No, I want to wait here!"

"As you wish. I do not think the hospital canteen is open at this hour but perhaps the nurse can get you a cup of tea. Please excuse me."

As the doctor went back into Mary's room Tom asked the nurse, "What is he going to do?"

"Mr. Page thinks that your wife is still bleeding internally. Her pulse is quite weak."

The nurse attempted reassurance.

"Don't worry. He is an excellent surgeon."

Tom had heard that assertion repeated twice before and it brought him no comfort. He stared at the empty bed for an hour after Mary had been wheeled away on a stretcher trolley. His despair grew as time went on without any news. The nurse who had brought him tea suggested that he take a stroll in the hospital grounds. Dawn was breaking and it seemed as if a fine day may follow. Tom was stiff from his night vigil and realised that stretching his legs was a sensible idea. The nurse told him that she would find him as soon as his wife returned from the theatre. He made his way to the hospital's main entrance and stood for a moment on the steps outside. Back at the farm his trusted employee would be attending to his usual duties in checking on all the livestock and providing them with food and water. Sam was a reliable, experienced farm hand, so Tom had no worries about his capabilities if left in charge. He would take care of Benjie, too. The thought that went through his mind was how quickly life can change from one day to another. Was it only yesterday that he was looking for the fox that was plundering Mary's chickens? It seemed a lifetime away. That safe, happy world that he and Mary had known had been destroyed in a moment of cruel callousness. Would life ever be the same for them again?

It was mid-morning before Mary was wheeled back into the intensive Care Unit. One look at the accompanying nurses solemn, unsmiling faces was enough to tell Tom that his worst fears would be realised. He stood aside as Mary was put back into the bed. Her breath was hardly detectable, her face as white as the coverlet placed up to her neck. The surgeon entered the room. Tom met his gaze and his heart sank.

"I am sorry, Mr Stearsby. She was so badly wounded. My team and I have done all we can to save her but I am afraid that you must prepare yourself for her loss."

Mary died late that afternoon. Tom stayed long after the monitor was switched off, holding her hand and still praying for the miracle that did not come. Finally, with his mind switched to automatic pilot, he found his way back home.In the days that followed his heartbreak would gradually turn to rage.

CHAPTER 7. RAGE

The story of the Post Office robbery and the double shooting dominated the front pages of the local press for several days. Any hopes that Tom may have had at being left alone to mourn the loss of his wife and unborn son were quickly and cruelly dashed.A small army of reporters and photographers parked themselves outside his cottage like a pack of hyenas scenting blood.They refused to leave until Tom showed himself at the front door. Benjie stood at his side barking furiously as cameras clicked and flashed.Tom told the press men he nothing to say and asked for privacy at a difficult time He suggested that they direct their enquiries at the police officer heading the investigation team.The firmness with which he closed the front door was an indication of his intention to answer no more questions and most of the journalist drifted off, possibly in the direction of the Post Office.The postmaster had been discharged from hospital but was convalescing at home.Tom doubted if he would give the newshounds much information about the robbery and his wife was still traumatised by the event.

Tom received a visit from the local constabulary who took statements about his personal life and his marriage.

He told them that he had inherited the farm from his late father who had died in a road accident.Tom had been born on the farm and had spent his childhood learning about husbandry and caring for livestock.He had known no other life but was quite content.After his mother died from cancer he extended the farm and increased the quality of the livestock.He had met Mary at a cattle show and was instantly attracted to her.They married within eighteen months.Life was fine with the couple looking forward to the birth of a child until the day of the raid on the local post office.Mary had been in the wrong place at the wrong time.That cruel act of fate destroyed all their hopes and dreams.

Mary's funeral was delayed because of the required post- mortem.When the county coroner finally issued the death certificate it confirmed that gun shots wounds were responsible for the deaths of the mother and unborn child. The same gun, a .38 calibre revolver,was also identified as the weapon fired at the postmaster.

If Tom had hoped for a small private funeral service in the local village chapel attended by members from the farming community with whom he had grown up,the publicity surrounding the killing of Mary ensured that it was not.On entering the cemetery gates behind his wife's hearse he was horrified to see a large throng had gathered outside the chapel. It was evident that the tragic event had attracted ghoulish onlookers from areas far beyond Cornchester.Two police officers were trying to keep order and prevent people trampling on graves in the church yard in their eagerness to surround the newly dug plot. Tom was so disturbed by the disrespectful scene that he found himself trembling from head to foot and needed support to get to his seat in the front pew of the church's pious interior. Struggling to control his breathing, he was conscious of the presence of some friends and neighbours and noted with some gratitude identifiable faces of nurses from the intensive care unit of the hospital. Beside them sat one of the two ambulance men who had attended Mary, the postmaster with his arm in a sling and two CID men who had interviewed him. Tom acknowledged them with a nod but his mind numbed again as Mary's coffin was carried down the aisle with quiet reverence. He scarcely heard the eulogy read out by the vicar, who recalled Mary's childhood in the village and her courtship and marriage to Tom. He recalled the wedding ceremony over which he had presided before declaring his revulsion at the violent act that had snatched away her life and that of her unborn child. The minister ended his eulogy with his firm conviction that God would make his own judgement on the responsible criminals and that justice would be served.

Tom stood at Mary's graveside for several moments after the rest of the congregation had departed. He stared with tear blurred vision at the flowers on top of the coffin. Behind him a small reverent group of friends shared his grief, though he was hardly aware of their presence. None of this was really happening. Tomorrow he would be back in the cottage with Mary, looking forward to the birth of their son and a happy future. He stayed with his mind in denial until he felt a hand firmly grasp his arm.He looked into the face of the vicar and was jerked back into dreadful reality.He was deluding himself!This was no nightmare from which he will awake.Mary is here, lying dead, with their son inside her. Hot rage welled up in his chest.If it was the last thing he ever did he would avenge these two innocent, precious lives.

CHAPTER 8. EARLY INVESTIGATION

Back at the farm Tom found it difficult to give his full attention to all the administrative matters connected to the efficient management of the land and the livestock. He left most of the care of the sheep and cattle to Sam and wandered desultorily from one task to another. It pained him to go through all the empty rooms of the cottage and not find Mary there.On the fourth day of aimless meandering he rang Cornchester police station and asked if there had been any success in finding the two men responsible for the post office attempted robbery.He was told that two detectives would call at the cottage and acquaint him with new developments in the case.

Tom rose early the next morning and impatiently awaited the arrival of the CID men.He listened as they gave him the information that had been provided by some of the witnesses to the robbery and the shooting.Both assailants were described as average in height and build and their ages estimated as between 30 and 40 years. Both had worn ski masks. The rest of their clothing was dark and not distinctive. The postmaster thought the man who had demanded the takings from the till and the wall safe spoke with a Northern accent. A black Ford Capri motor vehicle stolen in Manchester two weeks previously was found burned out a few miles from Cornchester two days after the post office theft. Though nothing in the Ford was identifiable the police took photos of footprints around the car in the hope that the footwear could be linked to the illicit drivers.

It was the next piece of information that interested Tom the most. The senior of the two detectives slowly opened a clenched fist to expose a small leather pouch. Inside was a black button engraved with the letters MN.

"This button was found in your wife's hand by one of the ambulance men who attended her after the shooting. It was given to the police sergeant who escorted you to the hospital. Your wife's clothing was checked and it did not match up with anything she was wearing. It looks like a button from a man's jacket. We believe that the letters MN stand for Merchant Navy. One of the witnesses said that when Mrs Stearsby was shot she fell towards the gunman with her hands held out. It is possible that as she fell she ripped the button from his coat. Of course, this is a long shot but one of the robbers could be or has been a seaman in the Merchantile Marine. In that case the button could be a vital piece of evidence."

The little leather pouch enclosing the button was carefully stowed away.

"We understand that your wife never regained consciousness from the moment she was shot. She never spoke in the ambulance. Can you confirm that she never spoke to you at all while you were with her in the hospital?"

Tom slowly shook his head; his mind back in the ITU, thinking of Mary's still white face.

"All right, Mr. Stearsby. Thank you. We will keep in touch with developments. Once again our sincere condolences."

After the two men had left, Tom sat pondering. He could not recall any mention of a button being found in Mary's hand but his mind had been so numbed by the tragedy that a lot of things that may have been said would have passed over his head. How much importance can be attached to a button, anyway? It was unlikely that Mary in her shocked state would have deliberately ripped off the button in order to provide a clue of the gunman's identity. And if the shooter had noticed that a button was missing from his coat it was probable that he would have destroyed the garment since then.

A month passed by. Tom tried to focus on his daily farming tasks but he could not clear his mind of the two men who were evading justice. Every day he hoped that he would receive news of an arrest. He considered leaving Sam in charge of the farm and begin a search for the two criminals. The problem was where to start. Neither had been identified. All he knew was that one of them apparently had a Northern accent and a stolen vehicle that may have been used in the robbery had been found burned out in the Manchester area.

The breakthrough came as his frustration grew to boiling point. A man was arrested ten miles away while attempting to rob a Post Office in the village of Perdsham. He was tackled from behind by a customer who was later identified as a local rugby player. The aborted thief was held in an armlock while the police were called. Enquiries revealed that his name was Peter Longhurst, a villain with previous convictions for assault and armed robbery. A search of his temporary abode brought to light a substantial amount of cash and a ski mask. Under pressure he admitted that he had been involved in the Cornchester post office robbery but denied that he had shot anybody. He named his accomplice as Len Wainwright. Police raided Wainwright's Newcastle home and found stolen goods, a cache of banknotes, a .038 calibre revolver and a black Merchant Navy jacket with a missing button. His girlfriend, a barmaid at the local Spotted Cow public house, said that she had not seen him for several days and did not know his whereabouts. A warrant was issued for his arrest. Police forces throughout the country were alerted to keep an eye open for him.

Tom Stearsby was contacted by Cornchester police and given the news of Longhurst's arrest. He fervently prayed for Wainwright's capture and vowed to be present at the trial of both men.

CHAPTER 9. TRIAL

Three months went by with Longhurst remaining in custody. The search for Wainwright widened when there were no sightings of him. His photograph from police records had been circulated all over the UK and international air and sea ports had been alerted. Interpol were requested to note any sightings of Wainwright and inform Scotland Yard. Despite all efforts the criminal remained unseen. It was decided by the Crown Prosecution Service to begin the trial against both accused of the same crime of armed robbery and involuntary manslaughter. In the case against Wainwright he would face justice 'In absentia" and had the right to appeal and demand a retrial if he was ever to be found and brought to court. This jurisdiction was explained to Tom. He expressed his pleasure that the trial would begin but he was not satisfied with the involuntary manslaughter charge or the right of Wainwright to demand a trial if he was captured. He needed to hear the 'guilty of murder' pronouncement by the jury on both accused men and see the black cap placed on the head of the judge. Even the alternative sentence of whole life without parole would not satisfy him. They had to pay with the loss of their own lives. If the court decided otherwise he would carry out his own form of justice.

Tom continued with his farming obligations almost automatically while rage surged through him. Each new arrival of a lamb or a calf deepened his grief of losing his wife and the baby son that she been carefully and proudly carrying through eight months of pregnancy. He spent many a night lying awake while each day his heart was wounded again with the birth of new young life on the farm. Any pleasure he had felt from the increase in animal stock was no longer there. The day of the trial could not come quick enough.

On the morning of the trial Tom arose earlier than usual after a sleepless night and prepared for a traumatic day ahead. If hIs plan was successful he would be unlikely to return to the farm that evening or for the foreseeable future. He had informed his senior stock hand of that eventuality and asked him to continue to manage the farm and all the livestock in the future. Sam had full access and authorisation to the farm accounts in order to draw his own wages and pay all bills relating to the farm and Wisteria Cottage.

Tom took Benjie for his exercise run and had a last inspection of his herd of dairy cows and the flock of sheep who were grazing in the fenced pastures. Everything seemed fine. Dealing with livestock was always an uncertain business but he hoped that it would not be necessary for his deputy to contact him with any problems. There would be no direct link between them in the near future. It was also certain that any telephone calls to and from the farm would be tapped by the police.

Returning to the cottage, Tom dressed quickly in the new black suit he had bought for Mary's funeral. He stared at his mirror reflection that was so unusual from his normal farmer's denims and heavy rubber boots. A tear slipped down his cheek as he had a stark mental picture of standing above Mary's coffin as it was laid into the grave. He cursed the two villains under his breath. At least one of them will pay the price today for the killing of his wife and his son. Whatever the verdict of the jury or the sentence pronounced by the Judge he would ensure that the deadly act would be fully avenged. He had been aware that the death sentence in England had been abolished but his rage burned so intensely within him that no other judgement would satisfy him. If he had to be the executioner then so be it.

Tom patted his terrier on the head and left him the kitchen knowing that Sam would soon be arriving and would care for him. The dog looked up at him with puzzled eyes but stayed standing as Tom walked out. The young farmer took one backward glance as he closed the main gates behind him. With Mary's death his life had changed forever. He did not know if he would ever return to the farm but he had a mission to avenge his wife and his unborn son and he would not come back to Cornchester until that mission had been accomplished. His throat tightened as he walked towards the town and the railway station. In his inside pocket of his coat was a photo of Mary looking into the lens of his camera, gleefully smiling at him with tender bright eyes. In his right hand, Tom tightly grasped a small brown leatherbound book of the Old Testament.

CHAPTER 10. SEAT OF JUSTICE

The train journey was uncomfortable. Tom rarely travelled by rail, always preferring to drive his old truck, but he did not know if he could park near the High Court in London. Even if he could do so, he did not want to be identified by the registration number of his vehicle if his plan of action went wrong. He preferred to remain anonymous, although he hated being among the mass of passengers waiting at the station and sitting in a crowded noisy compartment.

Although it was early morning there was the usual hustle and bustle of people going about their business in the City. Tom was unfamiliar with the Metropolis and he had never been in the vicinity of Westminster. He began to regret not driving his truck when pressed on other side by impatient Tube users on the escalators who seemed to have more urgent business than himself. It was with relief that he finally exited at Westminster Station. After checking the time on the wristwatch that Mary had bought him but rarely wore, Tom made another unusual gesture. He waved down a cab, which disregarded him and drove on. It took two more attempts before a taxi pulled up and a cockney voice asked,

"Where do to you want to go, Guv'nor?"

"The Old Bailey," Tom replied.

"Cor, blimey! You must be new in town! You are practically on top of it! Never mind. I will take you. Climb in."

Tom was deposited at the imposing entrance to the

Old Bailey by the cab driver who held out his hand for the small fare while remarking;

"Here you are, mate, but if you are attending one of the sessions they don't open the doors until 10 am.You will have to wait outside for another ten minutes or so.Are you a witness or somethink?"

Tom shook his head but merely said "Thank you," and climbed out. The Cockney glanced at him curiously before taking off the hand brake and driving away.

With time to spare, Tom examined the Portland stone of the Old Bailey's exterior and the three prominent sculptured female figures at the entrance. The cowled central figure known as the Recording Angel was flanked either side by the sculptured representations of Truth and Fortitude.Tom gazed with some awe.Higher up in relief panels TRUTH stood with a sword and a book of law in hand, while the other female figure held a quill and a journal.There were two other figures representing Spring and Autumn.The accompanying words were, 'As you sow,so shall ye reap.'

Tom took a step backwards. 200 ft above him the stern Roman figure of Justice stood on top of the great dome of the building. This gilded draped female Amazon carrying a sword in one outstretched arm and an evenly balanced pair of scales in the other weighed over 230 tons.Under her feet was a globe of the world.Tom was inspired to believe that the grim figure would see that Justice would be done in Mary's case.

A hand on his own shoulder prompted him to turn around. It belonged to Chief Inspector Murray, who was the head of the investigation team of the Cornchester robbery and the unlawful shooting of Mary and the Postmaster. One look at the Officer's grave face told him that he would hear bad news.

CHAPTER 11. DETERMINATION

"Good morning, Mr Stearsby. I am glad that you have decided to be present at the trial. You will be aware that after a conference with the Prosecution and the Defence lawyers the charge against Longhurst and Wainwright has been reduced from homicide to involuntary manslaughter. There is no evidence to prove that either of the two men deliberately set out to kill your wife. She just happened to be in the way when the Post Office was robbed. However, in extreme cases a life sentence without parole can be given for manslaughter and in this case the charge of armed robbery can also be added. All we can hope for now is that both charges are proven and a long prison sentence awaits both men. As you know, Wainwright is still at large, and the case against him will be heard in his absence. If convicted, he is still entitled to appeal and demand a retrial when he is captured."

Tom was not about to reveal that it made no difference to him what the verdict would be. He had his own plan of action. Both men would pay for killing Mary and his son with their own lives, no matter how long it would take. His words in reply to Murray's explanation of the reduced charge was emphatic.

"Wainwright and Longhurst both have previous convictions for armed robbery. They held up the Post Office at Cornchester armed with a gun and seriously assaulted the Postmaster before trying to escape. My wife was killed during that attempt. Who can prove that she was not deliberately shot because she was in their way?"

Murray sadly shook his head.

"Even if we caught Wainwright he is unlikely to confess that it was he who fired the gun or that it was his intention to shoot Mrs Stearsby. He is likely to say that the gun went off accidentally. It would be difficult to prove otherwise. Mr Stearsby, all the evidence will be heard in court and we must let the jury decide. The law must take its course and we must abide by that decision. Any previous criminal records have no relevance in this case. The jury cannot be swayed by that and can only make judgements on the evidence presented to them. Now, let us go inside and allow the trial to proceed."

Tom shook his head in bewilderment. The technical legalities of the case were beyond him. All he wanted was justice for Mary. Reluctantly he followed the Chief Inspector through the Great Hall into No.1 court. There were 18 courts in total but it was here that the most serious criminals were put on trial. Doctor Crippen and

Christie were among those who were tried and found guilty in court No.1 leading to their execution.Tom hoped that Longhurst and Wainwright would be added to that list,though their executions while justifiable, may be outside the present laws.

The Great Hall's ornate splendour impressed everyone who walked through it.Tom was no exception even though he was impatient to see Longhurst in the dock.Curved arches soared above his head and all around the walls were allegorical paintings depicting Labour, Art, Wisdom and Truth. Ornamental oak doors led to separate rooms for Lawyers, Barristers and witnesses.Judges had their own dining rooms.The most impressive sight seen from the centre of the marbled floor was the huge dome,above which Justice stood firmly in place surveying the world around her.Everything she stood for was evidence in her posture: power, authority, equity and impartiality. The Old Bailey was her domain,though it had changed many times over the years.It had been built on the site of the old Newgate Prison but Its name originated from the fortified wall built around London by the Romans.

Inside No.1 court, the trial jurors were already being selected and sworn in.Each were checked for their impartiality and confirmed that they had no previous acquaintance with the accused or any of their friends or relatives.None had personal knowledge of any of the defence and prosecution witnesses. Given those assurances,twelve adults were accepted by the barristers and took their places on the jury bench.Tom observed that there were seven men and five women, each looking rather nervous.It was not known if they had read any newspaper reports of the robbery but the press had been requested to give only limited details of the attempted theft and the following events which led to the death of a female.The identification of the two suspects and their previous criminal records were given only very brief coverage:insufficient for any reader to form a personal opinion as to their guilt or innocence in this case.It was the duty of lawyers to provide the evidence of that through their interrogation of the accused and the witnesses and convince the jury to bring the rightful verdict.Tom prayed that they would do so as he was directed to the public gallery by the clerk of the court.

Looking down from his high position,Tom was pleased to see that the dock was just below him in plain sight on his left-hand side.Longhurst would be facing away from him so he would be unable to see the facial expressions of the accused as he had hoped but he was close enough to hear the tone of voice used in reply to questions put to him. Any hint of arrogance or disdain would confirm that Longhurst had no feeling of remorse for his actions on that fateful day.Whether or not he fired the shot that killed a young farmer's wife and child was irrelevant.He had shared a common purpose with his absent conspirator in the Post Office robbery and was jointly responsible for the series of events which followed.

Tom watched the arrival of some of the witnesses escorted by their lawyers.He noted the limping figure of the Postmaster, still recovering from the serious injuries inflicted on him but determined to give an account of the robbery and the personal assault. His wife Sheila sat down beside him looking concerned with one arm locked in a tight embrace around his waist.

Six eyewitnesses to the robbery inside the post office and out in the street during the shooting came into the court with their counsel. Tom recognised one of them as the owner of the local hardware store where he had occasionally bought farming tools. The other identities were unknown but he presumed that they were either locals who was in the post office collecting their pensions or transacting other matters when robbery occurred. It subsequently transpired that three of the six willing to give evidence had been inside the store while the other three were onlookers on the street who had seen the thieves escape and heard the shot that killed the pregnant woman. All six had been close enough to Longhurst and Wainwright to identify them.

Those inside the Post Office had stood in shocked silence as Wainwright pointed a handgun at the postmaster and demanded the takings in the till. They continued to watch as the manager bravely stood his ground and grappled with the armed robber for the possession of the pistol. His wife had screamed in horror at the sound of the weapon being fired and buried her head in her hands; fortunately for her husband the bullet slammed through the soft flesh of his shoulder and into the wall behind the counter. It was later dug out and checked against the gun that was found in Wainwright's home after he had been identified. The rifling on the bullet extracted from Mary's body proved it was the same firearm.

The hustle and bustle in the courtroom ceased as the clerk called everyone to order and motioned them to rise as the robed and bewigged figure of the presiding judge appeared from his private chambers behind the Bench. He took his seat with appropriate solemnity and gazed around. Everyone except the legal team of lawyers resumed their seats. With one authoritative finger the judge beckoned them forward. A few minutes of whispered exchange took place before he apparently became satisfied with the replies they gave to his questioning and sank back into his chair. The lawyers returned to their respective positions with their witnesses. In the holding cell below the court Longhurst was released and escorted up to stairs which led directly to the Dock. Tom looked down expectantly. At last he would see one of the men responsible for Mary's death. Would he deny being present at the scene of the crime? Would he deny any involvement in Mary's demise and would he blame his accomplice for the killing? Would he adopt an arrogant attitude to all the accusations? The thought of that occurring filled Tom's mind with more hate and rage.

CHAPTER 12. EVIDENCE

Longhurst's physical appearance caught Tom by surprise He had expected to see a burly figure emerge.Instead, he saw a slim individual about 5ft.11inches in height.From his overhead position he estimated the age of the accused was in his late forties.The greying of hair above his ears and the beginning of baldness of his scalp suggested that he was no longer a young man.His face was featureless except for a large mole on his right cheek close to his thin upper lip.He stood in the dock and gazed with a look of contempt.It was clear that he had no respect for law or for anyone whose duty it was to uphold it.He continued to stare ahead as the charges of armed robbery and involuntary manslaughter were read out by the clerk of the court.As he was asked whether he pleaded guilty or not guilty his tone of voice sounded like a sneer.

"Not guilty."

Up in the gallery, Tom tightened his grip on the small leatherbound volume of the Old Testament.

The Postmaster was called into the witness box. After confirming his name and occupation he was addressed by the Prosecuting lawyer with the request to give a full account of the events that occurred in the Post Office on the day of the robbery.He did so in a clear voice which faltered slightly when it came to the personal assault, but he quickly regained his composure and gave a description of both his attacker and his accomplice who was wielding the firearm. He remained firm during the Defence barrister's questioning and emphatically denied that his memory and state of mind could have been impaired by the trauma of the robbery.The following witnesses who were present inside the Post Office were more hesitant in their replies to the Defence questioning but confirmed Longhurst's identity and his assault on the Postmaster.Shown photographs of Wainwright,they agreed that he was the armed accomplice.The three onlookers outside the post office who were called as witnesses to the two thieves escape from the premises and heard the shot that severely wounded the pregnant woman,later identified as Mrs.Mary Stearsby,were confident of the identity of the two men but were unable to establish if she was the deliberate target.Under questioning they admitted that there was a lot of confusion during the escape attempt and possibly the gun was fired in order to clear the getaway.

Tom sat listening to all the evidence with growing doubts in his mind.What would the jurors be thinking? His alarm heightened as the defence team seized on the possibility of the gun being fired accidentally.It became their main argument in attempting to persuade the jury to reject the manslaughter charge and only consider the robbery accusation.Whatever verdict was reached would not change his plan of action but the legal affirmation of guilt would have eased his mind that he would be applying justice in killing the pair.He watched the jury file out of court into an adjoining chamber to deliberate on the evidence Longhurst was taken back to the holding cells. Tom sat back on his seat and wondered how long he would have to wait before the jury returned and the prisoner was back in the Dock. Not that it mattered. He turned over the small book in his hands. The Day of Judgement had arrived.

CHAPTER 13. RETRIBUTION

The jury returned two hours later. Longhurst was brought back into the Dock. The Foreman stood up and with an expressionless face gave a majority guilty verdict on both charges. Tom closed his eyes with relief. His conscience was now clear. The judge looked intently at the Longhurst and pronounced sentence on both accused. Longhurst received fifteen years and the absent Wainwright received 25 years for the use of the gun in the robbery and the intentional shooting outside the court which ultimately cost the lives of a young female bystander and her unborn son.

With the court cleared and Longhurst taken in handcuffs back to await transport to prison, Tom left the Old Bailey and walked around to the side alley known as Dead Man's Walk. It was cold and gloomy with dusk beginning to fall but Tom felt calm as he prepared to wait for the prison van to arrive from the back entrance to the court. The sentences on the two accused were insufficient. They were not even life sentences. The Jury's Guilty verdict gave him justification for what he was now going to do.

Tom stood for nearly two hours before the prison van

arrived outside the court entrance and waited for the emergence of Longhurst handcuffed and escorted by two police constables. He waited until the prisoner and escort approached the rear of the van and then quickly advanced them from the gloom of the alley. They were unaware of his presence until he was almost upon them. All three stared at him as he opened the small volume of the Old Testament and extracted a Stanley knife that was nestling inside the hollowed-out pages of the religious book. He opened the sharp blade and with one quick movement slashed at Longhurst's throat. Blood immediately gushed out from the cut jugular vein. The prisoner's eyes widened in horrified amazement for an instant before slumping to the ground. The two police escorts, still handcuffed to the prisoner, were dragged down with him.

Tom stood impassively down at them as blood formed a puddle around his feet. The two guards tried to struggle to their feet but were prevented by the prone figure who was lying dead between them. The van driver, horrified by the scene he had just witnessed, finally jumped out of the vehicle with a police baton raised. Tom took one step back as the driver cautiously unlocked the handcuffs and allowed the escorts to get to their feet. They stared unbelievingly at the dead man and then at Tom, who dropped the Stanley knife to the ground. He made no other movement when all three uniformed policemen grabbed him by the arms and forced his wrists together behind his back, using the bloody handcuffs that had been on the dead man. Tom made no resistance as he was led away. His only thought was of a job half done. One down, one to go.

CHAPTER 14. ABSOLVEMENT

Tom was later remanded in custody and in accordance with English law made a first appearance at a Magistrates court. The stipendiary magistrate declined to make a judgement on a possible murder case and forwarded it on to a Crown Court. Transferred to Pentonville Prison, Tom endured the harsh conditions with quiet equanimity, quite content that one of the men responsible for the death of his wife and unborn son had received vengeance. Sooner or later, he would deal with the other.

Tom received some sympathy from prison warders who had read about his loss and interviewed by the Governor, he listened in silence to a lecture about the folly of taking the law in your hands and the resulting punishment for doing so. However, he was allowed to make a short telephone call to Sam to acquaint him of his present situation. His farm employee assured him that there was nothing he had not been able to deal with. Like Tom, he had been farming all his life and was capable of tending all the livestock. If necessary he could call for veterinary aid. He also informed Tom that he had read about the slaying of Longhurst, since it had received full coverage in the local newspapers and the national press. Tom hoped that wherever Wainwright was hiding he may also have read of the death of his accomplice. As brutal a man as he may be, he may have felt some nervousness that on his release from prison Tom would also hunt for him in order to exact revenge. Tom gained some slight pleasure from that thought.

Three months after his confinement in Pentonville, during which time Tom became a brooding solitary figure, the date for his trial was set. A defence lawyer was appointed who advised his client that he should plead not guilty on the grounds of diminished responsibility. The loss of his wife and unborn child had resulted in an unstable state of mind. Though the killing of Longhurst may have been premedicated it occurred because of the intense pain and hurt of his bereavement. Tom accepted the advice. If, as a result of this plea he was given a shorter sentence, all the better, but he remained determined to see Wainwright pay for Mary's death. With police forces throughout the country involved in the search for the wanted gun man and Interpol on the alert, it was logical to assume that his whereabouts would be traced and lead to his arrest. He had already been found guilty in his absence and received a long prison sentence but that did not satisfy Tom: he had been made aware that Wainwright could appeal and demand a retrial when he was captured ad returned to court.

The copy of the Old Testament that had carried the knife which Tom had used to kill Longhurst had contained two specific edicts which he had read and memorised. The book of Hebrew scriptures belonged to Mary, who had been given it by her grandparents who had been orthodox

Jews born in Tel Aviv, Israel.They emigrated to England and became part of the Jewish-Christian community.Their only child,a daughter named Martha, married a gentile and gave birth to Mary.Originally written in Hebrew and Greek the ancient scripture had been translated into English.Among the pages Tom had cut out to allow the insertion of the Stanley knife was the chapter of Exodus. It provided the justification for his killings of both men for the death of his wife and son. He could recite word for word the verses 21 to 25.

'If any men strive and hurt a woman with child so that her fruit departs from her he shall be severely punished according as the woman's husband lays upon him,and if any mischief follow then thou shalt give life for life, eye for eye, tooth for tooth, hand for hand, foot for foot."

Vengeful retribution or reciprocal justice is also part of Babylonian law as seen in Numbers 35 of the Old Testament.

"Someone found guilty of negligent manslaughter may be killed by a relative of the deceased who takes the role of the redeemer of blood."

Tom did not feel that any further justification for the killing of the two men responsible for the loss of his wife and baby was necessary but he was pleased that such edicts existed.He was just a country boy at heart and never believed that violent behaviour was acceptable; this was a different matter however.His hate and rage consumed him with such intensity that he knew that he would never be satisfied until Mary had been avenged with the deaths of the men responsible for her loss.Their world had been destroyed: their hopes and dreams of a happy future with a young son blown apart in an instant by one callous act.It did not matter if Mary and the baby were killed deliberately or not or whichever of the two armed robbers fired the fatal shot: the woman he loved would always be absent from his life and his son would never grow up.

CHAPTER 15. PROVOCATION

Tom's trial was held three months after his remand in Pentonville. At the pre-trial hearing his lawyer had argued that because the accused was of good character and posed no threat to the general public he should be released on bail.His crime was committed during a temporary period of extreme mental stress due to death of his wife. It was not a violent cause of action that would be repeated. As Tom stood before the magistrate listening to his counsel's plea with his head bowed in an apparent repentant posture he was thankful that his mind could not be read.It was true that he posed no threat to the general public but there remained a certain individual who had yet to pay for his crime.

As he expected,the plea for bail was rejected.Although the law states that every accused is accepted as innocent until it is proved otherwise, the charge of murder disallowed bail. His defence lawyer would have been aware of that fact, so Tom was grateful that he had made an attempt to gain his client some temporary freedom. It would have been nice if he could have returned to Wisteria Cottage and been welcomed by his dog Benjie and Sam. Tom would have also liked to have had the opportunity to thank his neighbours and friends for their steadfast support following the death of Mary. Those farmers who owned several hundred acres of land around the village would gladly watch out for Wainwright if he appeared within their precincts. He was unlikely to do so but the possibility existed. Descriptions of him had been circulated all around the village and the surrounding area. Anybody who thought they had seen him were asked to report the sighting immediately to the local constabulary.

Tom found himself back at the Old Bailey, but this time he was not in the public gallery. He was in the holding cell and brought up to stand in the dock. The presiding judge was already on the bench and the jury had been sworn in. In response to the clerk of the court's enquiry if he pleaded guilty or not guilty to the murder charge Tom glanced at his black gowned barrister before pleading 'Not Guilty.'

The Prosecutor stepped forward and called his first witness. It was one of the police officers who had escorted Longhurst from the court to the prison van. Tom did not recognise him. All his concentration had been on the handcuffed figure of the convicted Longhurst. He listened while the officer gave his testimony and identified Tom as the attacker.The other escorting officer and the police van driver followed him into the witness box and corroborated their colleague's evidence.Tom's barrister stayed silent. There was nothing to challenge at this point.The evidence given was indisputable.

The prosecutor stepped nearer the jury box and held out two hands.

"Ladies and gentlemen.Here is the proof that the accused standing in the Dock is not only guilty of murder but his attack on the victim was carefully planned and premedicated.I have here a Stanley knife used by the accused and a copy of the Old Testament in which the weapon was concealed.Both were recovered from the scene of the crime. If you are not familiar with the Stanley knife it a well-used cutting tool in the workplace with a very sharp retractable steel blade.I will demonstrate how it the blade is slid out before retracting it and handing to the usher.Please make no attempt to expose the blade.I do not want any injuries to occur.The book of the Old Testament has been deliberately hollowed out to conceal the knife.It was taken from the accused after the murder took place.It will also be passed along to you for examination.Whatever the Defence team may tell you in their argument on behalf of the accused there is no doubt of the intent to kill.Your verdict can be no other than guilty. I rest my case."

The two items of evidence were handed to the usher who gave them to the jury foreman.The judge indicated that he also wished to see them and received a nod of agreement from the usher.

There was a hush from the gallery as the Defence barrister stood up. The reporters in the Press box turned over to new pages in their notebooks in readiness for his opening words. The stenographer glanced up briefly as he passed her desk He waited while the two items of evidence were handed to the judge. He needed the full attention of the jury.

"Members of the jury," he began.

"From the evidence just presented you may believe that this is a prima facie case. That is not so. I will not dispute any of the facts that occurred at the scene of the crime and the man in the dock has been rightly identified as the person responsible for the killing of the victim named as Stephen Longhurst. The Stanley knife and the book of religion have been correctly accepted as belonging to the accused. What has not been established is the mental state of the man in the dock at the time of the alleged murder. The charge against him is incorrect. The indictment should have read 'Involuntary manslaughter with diminished responsibility'. In other words when the mind is disturbed because of previous incidents. This is a mitigating factor that needs to be examined. Allow me to explain and give relevant and substantiated facts of the circumstances which has led the accused to appear before you. The prosecution team may not want you to hear it but you have the right to do so."

He glanced at the presiding judge for approval, who took a few moments before issuing the warning.

"Do not divert from facts relevant to this case or

provide hearsay evidence.I will allow you to proceed in the interest of justice but do not stray beyond the legal boundary."

The defence barrister turned back to the jury.

"The man in the dock,whose fate will be decided by yourselves after your deliberations,is a widower. Your judgement should not be affected by that,but the circumstances which caused it is relevant to this case. Some months ago,in this very court,a man, together with an accomplice,was found guilty of armed robbery and the manslaughter of a pregnant woman and the child she was carrying in her womb.That man was the man slain by the accused standing in the dock."

Audible gasps were heard from two of the female members of the jury,echoed by a woman in the public gallery.

Tom's defending counsel continued.

"My client has pleaded not guilty to the charge of murder on the grounds of extreme provocation.That is not a plea than can be accepted by any court in the land.He will not refute the killing or deny that it was intentional.There is evidence that he planned his actions very carefully.The question you have to decide is his state of mind when he carried out the killing.Is it not reasonable that he was in such a state of grief at his loss of his wife and unborn child that he was beyond thinking rationally? That is for you to decide."

From the pocket of his gown the barrister produced some torn pages of printed text and held them up.

"'These pages were retrieved from the accused at the scene of the alleged homicide. He tore them out from the copy of the Old Testament that he always carried with him and in which he concealed the Stanley knife. I am offering them as evidence that the accused was influenced by the doctrine in Exodus and Numbers 35 when his mind was already unstable because of his intense feeling of grief. Those words motivated him to take the actions that have brought him into this court.

In the chapter Exodus of the old Hebrew testament, verses 21 to 25 proclaims that if any men strive and hurt a woman with child so that her fruit departs from her he shall be severely punished according to what the women's husband lays upon him, and if any mischief follows then thou shalt give life for life, eye for eye, tooth for toth, hand for hand, foot for foot.

I also ask the jury to note the dogma in Babylonian law about the right to take vengeful retribution.

I quote: 'some-one found guilty of negligent manslaughter may be killed by a relative of the deceased who takes on the role of the redeemer of blood.'

In a moment of temporary insanity the accused accepted that these precepts gave him the moral authority to administer reciprocal justice on the men responsible for the death of his wife. Since his arrest the accused has received psychiatric treatment which is still ongoing. I ask the jury to reject the First Degree murder indictment and find the accused not guilty."

There followed some cross examination of witnesses and a short closing argument by the prosecutor counsel rejecting the plea of temporary insanity.

"The killing of the victim was a deliberate,well planned attack. There is no proof that the accused mind was impaired when the violent act was committed.On the contrary it was skilfully executed.There can be no doubt that it was a deliberate act of murder."

The jury filed out and were escorted by the usher into a separate chamber to begin their deliberations. Four hours passed by before the Foreman announced that a majority verdict of guilty had been reached.Tom was brought back into the dock and awaited his fate.The judge gravely announced the verdict but then stated that sentence would be suspended until he had read all the psychiatric reports.Tom would be held in custody until then.The court would remain in session though the jury would be dismissed.The following day Tom was sentenced to twelve years in prison and was transported to Pentonville Prison in north London.

CHAPTER 16. IMPRISONMENT

Pentonville proved to be a dilapidated, vermin infected hellhole that was overcrowded with prisoners and despairingly lacking in the number of competent, qualified warders. Cells were small in size and cheerless. Toilet facilities consisted of slopping out bowls which had to be emptied every morning. Security was poor: there had been many previous escape attempts. That fact pleased Tom. Some had been successful through various means. Many prisoners had been recaptured within hours. Tom did not intend to be one of them. He had not been considered a high security risk although he had been convicted on a murder charge and been placed in A Wing which accommodated prisoners who had committed the most serious crimes. It had been accepted by his Honour at the Old Bailey that his crime was due to extreme provocation because of a preceding set of events which had caused him to lose self control. He was unlikely to kill again and he posed no threat to anyone else.

Tom found himself sharing a cell with a prisoner named Frankie Stevens, a habitual criminal who had spent most of his life behind bars. In a cell no more than 13ft in length and 7ft in width. It was inevitable that they were always in close contact with each other, but they shared no common interest and rarely conversed. It was a relief for both of them to be put to manual work outside during most of the daylight hours stripping tarry ropes in order to produce oakum. This was a fibre used for caulking wooden deck planks on ships.During this tedious task Tom spent most of his time scanning the outer walls of the prison looking for weak spots.

Back in his cell he made a sketch of the prison and the Exercise Yard. He had specifically noted the location of the old penal treadmill and the hollow shaft it was attached to.The treadmill,known also as a revolving staircase,was a form of punishment which could be operated by several convicts at a time but had been banned since 1898.Tom thought it could provide a means of escape.

Several weeks went by.Tom made use of the prison library and took maps of the local area back to his cell and studied the geography of the surrounding landscape. He also learned that under the prison was a very ancient trackway which dated back 6000 years.Here, too,was another possible escape route.In the Neolithic age, wooden planks of oak had been laid end to end on top of peat supported by crossed piece of oak or ash to form a stable walkway for man and beast to link fens across the marshes. London or Londinium, as Romans knew it, was a city built on marshland.These ancient trackways can be found throughout the world.

Tom studied the walls of the exercise yard.Several prisoners had made attempts to scale them.In consequence barbed wire had been attached on top.He would need protective clothing to scramble over them.He thought about the chapel to which all prisoners were escorted on Sunday mornings.The high stained glass windows on the rear wall above the altar rose clear of the outer prison wall. It would be an act of sacrilege to smash one of them but desperate men do desperate things. The doubt in Tom's mind was whether he could leap from the smashed window to the top of the outer wall and how big a drop to the ground there would be on the other side. He was quite athletic but any limb injury he may sustain would impede him and make recapture a distinct possibility.

Tom mulled over all these possible escape routes without reaching any definite conclusion. Life was simple back at the farm, living with Mary and tending to his animals. He had been born and bred in the country and knew no other life except farming. Husbandry management came naturally to him and he made decisions based on the welfare of his stock. He was now in a completely different environment and he hated it.

Sam came to see him during the allowed once weekly visits in a room put aside for that purpose and acquainted him with the condition of the livestock. They talked at length about various farming matters and Tom expressed his thanks for all Sam's efforts. Suddenly he leaned across the table where they were sitting opposite each other and lowered his voice so that he was out of earshot of the guard standing by the doorway.

"Sam. I need around £500. I know visitors are checked over for concealed weapons or drugs before they are allowed to enter but I do not think that there will be any concern that you are carrying that amount of cash. Try to hide it if you can and do not let yourself be seen handing it over. If it is found it may be considered that I wanted it to bribe prison officers."

Tom was about to continue when he noticed the guard raise his baton and gestured that he should sit back in his chair. Tom sank back but not before whispering to Sam,

"I have no living relatives now. The farm will belong to you when I have gone."

He knew that he would require additional help when he finally escaped He hoped that his remark would be an added incentive. Sam was an honest man and would not easily be persuaded to act unlawfully, even for his boss.

CHAPTER 17. BREAK OUT

Tom spent a restless night with troubled thoughts disturbing his sleep. In the lower bunk Frankie Stevens heard his mutterings and cursed his incoherence. No doubt his cellmate was an oddball but if he was thinking of a way to escape from this hell hole he wanted to know what he was scheming. He was unaware that Tom's distressed mental images of Mary lying so still in the hospital had by the end of the night deepened his resolve that Wainwright would meet the same fate as his accomplice.

Tom was pleased to receive a visit from the Cornchester postmaster, who was back at work after security had been tightened at the post office with the installation of a metal grille at the counter. He told Tom that his wife was still traumatised by the attempted robbery and would not attend alone to customers. Police had no luck in tracing Wainwright but the arrest warrant was still in force. The Post Office manager also assured Tom that if he ever needed help with any personal or business affairs he would be more than willing to help.

During the next visit of relatives and friends to Pentonville the exchange of cash from Sam to Tom was successfully arranged due to an altercation between one of the other convicts and his wife which needed the guard's intervention. By the time the couple had been separated and the wife escorted out the transfer had taken place. The envelope containing the 50 £10 notes nestled against Tom's abdomen inside the brown prison garb worn by prisoners. Visits were cut short because of the scuffle and prisoners were taken back to their cells without the normal checks carried out by the guards.

Six months later, Tom made his escape. It was surprisingly easy. Dysentery broke out due to the unhealthy conditions in the prison cookhouse and the lack of hygiene shown by the staff in preparing the food. Most of the prisoners and warders were affected and the small prison hospital could not cope with the number of patients. Those affected with bloody diarrhoea and acute abdominal pain were transferred to a local civil hospital. Tom suffered mildly but faked his symptoms as being more severe and was included. His cell mate Frankie Stevens went with him, determined not to let Tom out of his sight.

CHAPTER 18. AVOIDING CAPTURE

In a long dormitory the pair were given beds close together after being given kaolin and antibiotics.There were no fit warders available to carry out their duty in guarding the convicts so the corridor was manned by two female nurses.In the middle of the night Tom very quietly left his bed and crept down the room, crouching on all fours as he passed the side room where the two nurses were sitting. He passed through the open door to a landing where stairs led to the ground floor.Behind him crouched Stevens.Tom glared him and hissed through gritted teeth.

"Go away! I don't want you with me!"

Frankie made no move.Tom was not about to argue. There was no-one else to be seen but they could be disturbed at any moment.He moved to the top of the stairs.One dimmed lamp showed a side entrance door which led to the ambulance bay. Slowly on tiptoe he crept down.He was followed by his cell mate. With his heart beating fast,Tom tried opening the door.It yielded outwardly. Resisting the urge to run,Tom stepped slowly outside. The stone steps felt cold under his feet. His thin night gown fluttered in the draught. Tom was thankful that he had taped the small envelope to his left underarm. The door behind him closed. Stevens stood behind him, gazing down at the row of unmanned ambulances.

"Let's go for F.... sake," he whispered, pushing Tom in the back.

They both edged forward, crouching low as they passed the emergency vehicles.They reached the open street.It was dark and unlit except for one lamp post.The moon was hidden behind clouds.Tom estimated that it was between three and four a.m. He had about two hours before dawn began to break but he had to hurry. He turned to Stevens.

"Sorry, chum,but I have things to do.You are on your own from now on.."

He did not wait for any protests but sprinted away. He knew that Frankie was older and less fit than himself. He would never keep up.When he reached the corner of the street two hundred yards away he glanced back.Stephens was still standing there, looking slightly bewildered.

CHAPTER 19. DISGUISE

In passing a group of terraced houses Tom noticed an assortment of garments on a clothes line in one of the back gardens. Unbolting the gate and creeping up the concrete path he found a pair of jeans,a man's shirt and jumper. By the back door was a pair of gardening shoes roughly his size. He discarded his prison nightgown,retrieved the cash envelope and dressed quickly in the selected clothes. Nothing fitted perfectly but they would do temporarily.

Tom walked about four miles before the sun began to rise in the East.It gave him a sense of direction.The place names of London suburbs meant little to him but he knew that he needed to head north east.He tried to keep off the main streets as much as possible.Back at the hospital the nurses would be checking on patients.Security guards would be called when the two empty beds in the corridor occupied by the dysentery sick patients from Pentonville were discovered.He had to move faster to get out of the capital before police forces were alerted.

Tom looked back at the increasing road traffic as early workers began their journey to their place of business. One or two of the car drivers looked at him curiously as they drove past.If police had checked any of them and asked if they had given a lift to a man in the early hours of the morning or had seen a man running alone, the police pursuers would consider the possibility that he was one of the escaped prisoners and make a concentrated area search. He began to jog but the gardening shoes kept slipping off his heels.He passed a primary school and on impulse vaulted the low boundary wall and ran round the back of the building.It was too early in the morning for the young children to arrive for lessons.He peered through the windows of empty classrooms.No sign of any teaching staff or a caretaker.He slumped down with is back against the brick wall. Suddenly he felt tired and very thirsty.His heels were forming blisters.

Tom sat with his eyes closed for a few minutes.His bout of dysentery had been mild but had left him feeling quite weak.He wished he could have rested for a longer period but he knew that he had to keep on the move.

He heaved himself upright and looked around. A sports pavilion stood at the edge of a small playing field. He made his way across to it and managed to wrench off the small padlock that secured the entrance. He used the toilet and the washbasin inside before opening several lockers. He found a pair of plimsolls that fitted him and he gladly discarded the gardening shoes. There was little else in the way of clothing that were of any use but he did find a small hand mirror and a hair comb that he pocketed. He exited the school from the back entrance knowing that he had left a trail of evidence that would confirm his presence.

Tom emerged into a quiet side street and continued in a north easterly direction until he came across a parade of shops which were just opening up. One was a small clothing store. Tom took a risk and entered it after removing the bank notes from the envelope in the jeans he taken from the house owner's garden. He selected a dark jacket, trousers, a blue shirt, socks, underwear and a pair of size eight shoes. He changed into them in the shop's small fitting room before asking the elderly proprietor him if he had a bag in which to put the clothes he had been wearing.

On leaving the shop he was again aware that he was leaving a trail behind him but it did not matter if he was traced to this little store. He hoped to be well outside of London by then. He strode with more confidence among the busy streets until he reached an open market with a number of individual owned stalls selling a range of retail goods. From one stall selling hair products he bought black hair dye and a pair of scissors. In the locked cubicle of the public toilets he cut his blond hair and dyed it black using the hand mirror and comb he taken from the primary school's sports pavilion. A pair of horned rimmed glasses completed his disguise.He examined his profile in the mirror and was satisfied it would pass muster.He was not used to wearing a hat but he would if need be.He bought a ham sandwich and a dubious tasting cup of coffee from a food stall and two hours later boarded a train at London Bridge.His third class ticket showed that his destination was Rothbury in Northumberland.

CHAPTER 20. NORTHWARD BOUND, SEEKING SUPPORT

During the five hour train journey to this historic market town on the north east coast,Tom sat and watched the miles roll by and contemplated on the chance he was taking.He had not spoken to Jenny since she had rung him to express condolences after reading of Mary's death but he was certain that she would be pleased to see him.She and Mary had formed a close friendship during their visits to Cornchester when he was buying his first herd of Dairy Shorthorn cows from her large farmstead. Whether she would support him in his endeavour to trace Wainwright was another matter.She was a wealthy woman, being the great niece of the renowned industrialist, scientist and inventor Sir William Johnstone, but she was also chairman of Rothbury District Council and would not do anything that would damage his or her reputation.

Tom changed trains at Morpeth and took the single track branch line to Scots Gap operated by Wansbeck Railway Company.From this small village,noted mainly for its annual agricultural mart where sheep and cattle were bought and sold,Tom continued on to the terminus at Rothbury,the medieval village on the River Coquet deep in the Simonside Hills. He had made this journey in reverse with Jenny Johnstone when he was buying livestock for his farm. It was a long way to travel from Cornchester to buy sheep and cattle but she was one of the top breeders in England who could be relied on to trade fairly and give sound unbiased advice and support to any potential purchaser. The Border Leicester rams and ewes he bought from her had been interbred with Merino sheep and had been the backbone of his flock.

Tom alighted at Rothbury,unknowing that the Prince of Wales, later King Edward VII,had made the same 13mile journey on the single track with his family in order to visit Peakview Manor,the former shooting lodge which had been extended by Jenny's great uncle into a large imposing house on the edge of a sandstone crag overlooking Northumberland County Park.It was not a train ride that many would make because it was a steep switchback with a dangerous curve that had caused many serious accidents. Its avoidance by those exploring the

Simonside Hills was another reason why Tom had decided to use the route.

Jenny's farmstead, spread over almost 500 hundred acres, lay a mile north of the village. Tom strode to it with his mind reflecting on his own farm and his livestock, wondering if Sam had found another labourer to help him out with the milking. Somehow he had to get word to him but he knew that he could not do that directly. All telephone calls to Wisteria Cottage would be monitored by the police. He hoped that Jenny could help as she was well connected all over the country.

He found her in one of the stables dismounting from one of her ponies. She looked at him curiously as he entered.

"You should not be here, whomever you are. This area is out of bounds for visitors. If you are here on business please go back to the house and wait."

Tom smiled and removed his false spectacles.

"Hullo, Jenny. It's me, Tom!"

She stared at him.

"Tom? Good grief! What are you doing here? I did not recognise you. What happened to your blond hair?"

She strode over to him, her slightly annoying look replaced by a frown. She kissed him on his cheek.

"Wait a minute. Let me put Bluebell away."

Tom watched as she removed the saddle and bridle

and stabled the pony.He still gazed at her as she took off her riding cap and shook her long auburn hair free. She was still a slim, graceful beauty even without make up.It was difficult to believe that she was in early sixties. She had never married.She had been engaged to a senior officer in the Northumberland Hussars who was killed in Crete a month before their planned wedding date. After his death she concentrated on farming and had spent her life breeding cattle and sheep,gaining both a fortune and a reputation for her knowledge and her humanitarian care for all animal life.

Linking an arm into Tom's own, she smiled up at him.

"Let's get back to the house.I need a drink and so do you by the look of you.It's lovely to see you but I want to know why you are here.You did not ring me in advance or else I would have been prepared."

Tom was silent for a moment before saying "It's a long story, Jen. I will tell you once we are inside."

"That's fine,Tom.We have not spoken since Mary's funeral so we have a lot to catch up on. I have been abroad a lot in the last year talking to other breeders and when I am here I am always involved with Council affairs."

Once installed in the large oak panelled lounge of the farmhouse Jenny poured out two glasses of wine and handed one to Tom before settling herself in a comfortable leather armchair.She beckoned Tom to sit opposite.

"Right,Tom.Bring me up to date.First things first.How

are things back on the farm? Anything wrong with the sheep or the cattle?"

Tom shook his head.

"Nothing's wrong with them, Jen.They are doing fine and have produced strong healthy lambs and calves.You sold me good stock.That is not why I am here."

Jenny smiled.

"That's good,Tom.It is not often I get complaints.You have come a long way to see me,though,so you must have a good reason."

Tom hesitated.He had never been deceitful but the less Jenny knew about the events that had occurred since Mary's death the better.He certainly could not tell her that he had escaped from prison.

"Jen, you may remember that two men were responsible for the robbery of the post office in Cornchester and that Mary was killed during their escape.You may recall that one of the men was captured and the other is still in hiding. The police are still hunting for him.They raided his house in Newcastle and found the gun and enough evidence to incriminate him but he seems to have vanished into thin air.I cannot settle until he is brought to justice and I have decided to search for him myself.My chief farmhand Sam is tending the livestock back at Cornchester until I get back.Your great uncle Sir William was born in Newcastle and I know you lived there as a child.You know the area well and you will have contacts with the local authority and with the police.If I asked them for help in catching the second robber they would refuse.They would tell me that while they understand my motive they cannot condone any action of mine in acting independently. All I would like you to do,if you are willing,is to check with the police chief at Newcastle if the search for the hunted man is still actively ongoing and what areas have been covered."

Jenny looked doubtful.

"I am not sure if I can help you,Tom,but I will have a private word with the Chief Constable and ask if there have been any recent developments.He may not be willing to tell me anything. However I am involved in Police funding in Northumberland so he may bear that in mind.What is the name of the wanted man, by the way?"

"Len Wainwright. He is a hardened criminal so his name will be on police records."

"What makes you think he may be here in the north?"

"His house in Newcastle was raided by police and they found incriminating evidence that he was involved in the Mary's shooting.They have not been able to trace him but they know he belonged to the Tyneside gang and they may be hiding him.My feeling is that he would not stay in that vicinity but would hide somewhere more isolated. Northumberland is a wild, forested county where a man could stay for years without being detected. I have a feeling he may be somewhere between here and the Cairngorms.I want to try to find him."

"All right,Tom,I will help you if I can but please bear in mind that I will not approve of any action by yourself in

JUST A SIMPLE COUNTRY BOY

taking the law into your own hands. If you find Wainwright's whereabouts you must immediately inform the police. You know I am a Justice of the Peace and leader of Rothbury County Council. I am in close contact with the Chief Inspector of Newcastle Police Force. I cannot be involved in any illegal activity."

Tom nodded. "I know that, Jen, and I would not want you to. I really want to know if there has been up to date developments in the search for Wainwright or any sightings reported of him."

"I will have a word with the Chief Constable. Now, where are you staying, Tom? You look worn out to me. I can give you a bed for the night if you would like to stay. Have you eaten lately? My cook will be preparing a meal for me soon. I will ask her to lay an extra place for you."

"Thanks, Jenny. That is kind of you. I am staying in Morpeth but I will be out and about so I think I will need to ring you to hear what information you have been able to get."

"No problem, Tom. If I am at a meeting I will leave a message with the maid. Now, how about another drink? You will not get a train back to Morpeth tonight."

67

CHAPTER 21. PREPARING FOR NORTHUMBERLAND CRAGS

The evening passed pleasantly with Jenny enjoying the unexpected company and the conversation which concentrated on her breeding experience.The wine and the comfort of the armchair had a very relaxing effect on Tom,who stifled a yawn that he could not completely hide from his hostess.She directed him to an en-suite bedroom where he embarrassedly confessed that he had no other clothes except those he was wearing. Jenny laughed.

"My senior stockman lives in a cottage behind the stables.He must have a spare pair of pyjamas. I will ring him and ask if you can borrow a pair.In the meantime, there is a shower with toiletries in the en-suite. Incidentally, the clothes you are wearing are ill suited for either the wild terrain or the harsh climate that we get here.I will see what I can find for you."

Tom showered,being careful not to get his dyed hair wet.In response to Jenny's enquiry for the reason of changing his hair colour and wearing spectacles he did not need,he explained that Wainwright knew that the husband of the woman he had shot would be seeking revenge.He had seen Tom's photo in the newspapers and would recognise him without some disguise. That would make it harder for Tom to apprehend him.

The following morning, Tom found a heavy waterproof jacket,a thick high necked lambswool sweater and a pair of stout hiking boots outside his bedroom door. He dressed quickly and went downstairs to thank the provider. Jenny was in the breakfast room helping herself from a bowl of steaming porridge. She looked at him approvingly.

"That's better, Tom. It is wild country out there. Very boggy in places and many rocky crags to clamber over. My advice to you is to forget all about this manhunt and go back home. You are a farmer, not a sleuth. You could spend all year searching for Wainwright and never find him. In fact it is madness. He could be anywhere in the country."

Tom nodded.

"I know, Jen. I just have a hunch he is up here somewhere. If I was back at Cornchester I could not settle knowing he is on the loose. He is a dangerous criminal and capable of doing anything that will help him to evade capture. So far, the police have been unable to track him down. I owe it to Mary to try to find him to bring him to justice. By the way, when you talk to the Chief Constable please do not tell him that I have been here or what my intentions are. I do not want you involved any more than you are already. Thanks, incidentally for the warmer clothing."

"Thank Alistair, my chief hand. They belong to him. He likes to go hiking and rock climbing on his days off. He has also left a spare rucksack. Now tell me, who is looking after your livestock while you are away?"

Tom told his hostess about his farm worker Sam whom he trusted implicitly, and they chatted while enjoying the Scottish oats and the bacon and eggs that followed. Tom again expressed his gratitude to Jenny for the help and support she had given him since he bought the cattle and sheep from her.The subject changed and he learned more about her great uncle Sir William Johnstone and the grand mansion called Peakview Manor,which he had built on the edge of a high rocky crag in Rothbury Forest. He had transformed a small shooting lodge in order to do so and had arranged the planting of seven million trees in the Simonside Hills which overlooked Rothbury.

Jenny was very proud of her great uncle and had gained much of her wealth through shared enterprises.Sir William became a very successful entrepreneur in the armaments and transport industry and had been rewarded with a barony.He founded the armaments firm Whitworth with engineer and designer Joseph Whitworth who had invented the first breech loading rifle.The company also became heavily involved in the aerospace industry and merged with Vickers in early aircraft production.Other forms of transportation soon followed.Ships and locomotives earned them a huge fortune. Johnstone also had a great interest in hydroelectricity and invented hydraulic machinery including giant cranes which benefited builders and manufacturers. Peakview became the first house in the world to use the power of water to provide the force to run domestic appliances.

Sir William also built dams and reservoirs in the 1000 acre estate around Rothbury and was a great philanthropist. He bought and gathered together a great art collection, buying masterpieces that he hung on the interior walls of his grand mansion. Jenny had inherited some of them which Tom had admired on her lounge walls.

After thanking Jennie for her hospitality, Tom hesitated before saying, "I know this is an imposition, Jen, because you have been so helpful already, but I came away without bringing my chequebook with me and I have practically run out of cash. Can you lend me a few pounds? It may be some time before I can pay you back."

Jenny smiled.

"That's alright, Tom. I know you are a man of integrity. Some of the farmers and breeders like to deal in cash so I have a certain amount here. Just wait a moment."

She exited the room but returned within few minutes with a bundle of bank notes in her hand.

"Here you are, Tom. Eight hundred pounds. That should be enough to pay for meals and accommodation for a while. If you need any more, please let me know."

Tom gratefully kissed her on her right cheek, briefly catching the scent of her perfume.

"Jenny, you are a sweetheart. Thanks so much. I will pay you back as soon as I can."

At the front entrance of the palatial farmhouse Tom picked up the black rucksack, shrugged it over his shoulders and kissed Jenny again. She stood and watched him go before giving him a last wave and disappearing back in the house.

Jenny had provided Tom with a map of the local area,

so he headed north towards Thropton.It proved to be a small, sparsely populated village two miles west of Rothbury and south of the highly elevated Tosson Hill at the edge of Simonside Forest. Close by was the ruined medieval Great Tosson Tower House.

In the Middle Ages this lawless Borderland between Scotland and England had been the scene of frequent skirmishes between the two nations.In addition to the military threat the civilian populace was also under attack by mounted gangs of armed robbers who became known as Border Reivers.Reiver is an old word for plundering. It also gave rise to the verb 'bereaved' and the noun 'bereavement'.The Reivers came from both sides of the Border and stole livestock and anything of value and were likely to kill anyone who showed any hostility. Watch Towers and fortified farmhouses known as Bastle houses were built as means of defence. Many of these buildings still exist, though mainly uninhabited and in a ruinous state.Great Tosson Tower was one of them.It was possible that Wainwright would make use of them as hiding places.Tom hoped to search many of them but also intended them to provide one or two as temporary accommodation for himself.While it was unlikely that the police would search Northumberland and Cumbria for him it was a possibility that local forces had been notified of his escape from prison.

CHAPTER 22. INTO THE UNKNOWN

In Thropton, Tom found a 300year old coaching inn called The Three Wheats, a small post office and a grocery store. He entered all three and produced an old newspaper photo of Wainwright and asked if anyone had seen him. He received negative replies. His next targets were the Pele Watch Tower and the disused lime kiln just outside the village. No signs of any occupation in either. He crossed the bridge of the River Coquet and made his way across a densely wooded path towards Holystone, pausing briefly at the small village of Sharparton to gaze at the sheep grazing in an open pasture. It took his mind back to his own flock and for an instant he wished he was back at Cornchester. He shrugged the thought aside. Finding Mary's killer and avenging her was the only way he would appease his hate and anger. However long it took, wherever he had to go he would hunt Wainwright down and make him pay for the loss of his wife and child. He turned away and continued down the track towards the village that dated back to William the Conqueror.

Tom had set his sights on the medieval village of Holystone, situated on the north bank of the River Conquet at the edge of Northumberland National Park and which lay beside an ancient Roman road. He was drawn to it by the significant landmark shown on his map of Holy Well, the priory home of Augustinian Canonesses, which was dedicated to St. Mary the Virgin in the first half of the 12th century. Sadly, the priory had been demolished in 1541 at the time of the Reformation but the ruins still remained beside the Holy well, known as Lady's Well. This is a deep-water tank fed by a natural spring and is the main source of water in the village.Tom briefly thought of it as the place for the disposal of Wainwright's body if he ever caught up with him but then dismissed the idea.He did not want to pollute the ancient well which served the local population. He was only interested in the death of one man.

Having scoured the small village and the ruins of the priory,Tom moved on through a densely wooded area to the village of Harbottle.On Jenny's map it showed the Motte and Bailey castle built by Henry II in 1160.Tom had heard of only one similar castle which was still inhabited by royalty and that was Windsor Castle in Berkshire.That had been built by the Norman King William in the 10th century and has survived until the present age. Motte refers to a natural or artificial mound upon which the fortification is built. Its purpose was to have a height where surrounding land could be observed for the approach of enemy forces. Bailey was the name of a walled courtyard built around the castle which could be manned for defence and which would hold all the explosives and weapons for the use of the garrison.These castles were originally built of wood until the 12th century and fell into decay over the years. Those built with brick inevitably suffered the same fate and their ruins can be seen throughout the country.Tom thought of the Old Bailey where he had been tried and remembered that the City of London was once surrounded by a defensive wall built by the Roman legions.

Harbottle had an interesting history, but Tom was only concerned by the possibility that Wainwright was in the vicinity or had passed through it.By the time he had checked the castle ruins and climbed up to the huge sandstone boulder on the hill known as the Drake Stone he felt very weary.He had read that the boulder was endowed with supernatural powers.He stood beside for it for a moment hoping that he would be granted paranormal vision to see Wainwright's location.The boulder remained motionless and silent.Tom laughed at his foolishness. Perhaps everyone was right.His mind was unstable, and he needed psychiatric help.This was an impossible task.The Northumberland National Park covered over a thousand kilometres with small villages and settlements scattered everywhere.The Cheviot Hills and the Keilder Forest still lay before him. He decided to book into the only public house in the village for a night or two. He had passed the small Star Inn on his way through to the castle ruins.With some sustenance and a good night's sleep, he may feel more refreshed and optimistic.

CHAPTER 23. AN UNEXPECTED TURN OF EVENTS

Tom spent the next three days walking through wild terrain thankful for the heavy coat and stout boots that Jenny had provided.Many of the villages and settlements in the Cheviot Hills that he wanted to check for Wainwright were accessed through boggy marshland or densely forested areas on mountainside. Unable to find suitable shelter at night he was forced to use some of Jenny's £800 on accommodation in the odd hostel he passed. On the fourth day of unsuccessful searching for his quarry he decided to ring Jenny to ask if she had spoken to the Chief Police Inspector at Newcastle about any possible sightings of Wainwright's location. Her angry response to his call took him aback.

"Tom, I could not believe what I was told. You completely deceived me! Inspector Burrows told me the whole story of your prison sentence for killing Longhurst and your escape with your cellmate. Not only that but the day after you left me Peakview Manor was burgled and some of my great uncle's art collection was stolen. Were you involved in that too?"

Tom was astounded by the last accusation.

"Jenny, of course not! I am not a thief. I would not steal from you or your uncle or anybody else. I am sorry that I deceived you but I could not tell you what really happened. You are a J.P. and you would have acted lawfully and insisted on my arrest. I needed to find Wainwright and get justice for Mary before handing myself in."

"Well, Tom. You can do that right now because your search is over. Wainwright is dead! He was one of the three robbers engaged in the burglary and slipped off a crag and smashed his skull on a rock while carrying one of the paintings. He was later identified from police records.One of the other two men turned out to be your former cellmate,Frankie Stevens.The third man has not been identified but I did think it may have been you.We talked about Peakview at breakfast before you left,if you remember? Anyway,Tom,whether or not you were involved in the burglary,I have lost all trust in you.Do not contact me again. Just give yourself in."

The phone went dead.Tom stood for a moment with it in his hands before putting it down.He was so astonished that he could hardly draw breath.Wainwright dead?Frankie Stevens up here in Northumberland?Her great uncle's mansion burgled? It was all too much to take in.He ordered a brandy from the hostelry bar and sat heavily in a chair to drink it.What now? He was sorry that he was not able to carry out his personal act of revenge on Wainwright but relieved that his search for him had come to an end.He had been completely out of his depth in this mountainous region and he was always conscious that he may feel a tap on his shoulder by a uniformed police officer standing behind him.That could still happen,but Jenny's news changed everything.There had to be a new game plan now.Frankie Stevens and the unknown accomplice in the Peakview burglary had to be found and dealt with before he could consider a return to his prison cell.Just as important was his relationship with Jenny.That had to be restored.

CHAPTER 24. A CHANGE OF DIRECTION

Tom was tempted to head east and get to Sir William's manor to find the exact place where Wainwright had met his death; but he reasoned that the area would be swarming with police hunting for the two other burglars. The former owner of the mansion had been a very prominent figure and benefactor in Northumberland and Tyneside although his home and much of his estate had been bequeathed to the National Trust on his death. Most of his valuable art collection had remained as an added attraction to tourists.The Chief Inspector of Newcastle police had been urged to devote as much manpower as he could afford to catch the thieves.Tom could be caught up in the net.He thought long and hard before reasoning that Stevens and his accomplices would want to hide their loot until they could sell it on to unscrupulous art dealers. Wainwright had been part of a criminal gang located in the Newcastle area and he would need their co-operation in selling on the stolen paintings.It seemed sense to be in contact with them but not close enough to be caught.Tom bought a local road map which included the East coastline from Amble down to Tynemouth.

Three days later Tom was in Amble.He had avoided Rothbury and Jenny's farmhouse and took a detour up through the forest to the little hamlet of Pauperhaugh, where he spent the first night in the ruins of an old Roman camp.On his map the place was appropriately called the Devil's Causeway. Waking cold,wet and hungry,he walked to the next village of Longframlinton and booked into the Granby Inn for a hot bath and breakfast. Handing over payment from Jenny's cache he had a moment of concern about their broken relationship. He knew that he was to blame for that rupture and he understood her anger. He would apologise and repay the £800 as soon as he had dealt with Frankie Stevens.

The hot bath refreshed him but he had to dress again in his damp clothing. Looking in a mirror, he viewed his appearance. He had grown a beard which needed trimming: his blonde hair was beginning to show through the black dye. He had to do something about that in the next town

The dining room was empty except for a young woman sitting at a table with a pram beside her. She looked up at him as he passed by to take his seat and half smiled. He nodded politely and said "Good morning!"

She half smiled again before turning to the pram and taking out a baby boy to feed him from a bottle of milk. Tom estimated that he was just a few months old. He had a sudden vision of Mary. He squeezed his eyes shut. The boy could have been his son! He clenched his fists before turning his head away and standing up.

The child's mother looked startled.

"Is something wrong? Can I be of assistance?"

Tom looked down at her and shook his head. "I am sorry. I am fine. I did not mean to frighten you or your son."

The young woman still looked concerned. Tom realised

that she was quite pretty.She watched as he walked towards the breakfast bar.It was obviously self-service.The counter had several covered dishes standing on a hot plate with a box containing cutlery beside a pile of crockery.Tom selected a bowl of porridge, bacon, sausage and a soft yolked fried egg,poured out a cup of coffee and returned to his table.He glanced across at the mother who was still holding the bottle of milk from which the baby was sucking.In front of her was a half empty dish of cornflakes.

"Have you had your breakfast?" Tom enquired. "Can I get you anything from the breakfast bar?"

"No, thanks. I am not hungry. It is little Timothy that needed feeding."

She looked across at Tom's full plate and added: "You should feel better after eating that! Have you come far?"

Tom lied and explained:

"I have been hiking throughout the County. I have probably overextended myself.It is quite heavy going in parts."

He noted her green eyes as she put the bottle away and placed the child over her shoulder to burp him before tucking him back in the pram. She leaned back in her chair and watched him eat.

"Yes, it can get pretty wild out there.You can get fatigued very quickly if you are not used to climbing the Marylins.At least you have not encountered any Duegars,it seems, as you have survived so far."

Tom swallowed a piece of Cumberland sausage before asking in a puzzled tone,

"Sorry, you have me there.What are they? I am from the South and this is my first venture up here."

She chuckled.

"You are a novice! A Marilyn is the name for any mountain with a prominence of over 150 metres or 492 ft.Named after Marilyn Monroe, of course.There are many in England.The highest peaks in Scotland are called Munros! As for Duergars, they are legendary,mythical dwarfs that apparently appear at night with torches in the Simonside Forest trying to lead hikers and walkers into traps, either falling into a bog or over a precipice.Not very nice people but they do disappear at dawn."

"Good heavens!" Tom exclaimed.

"I will certainly watch out for them! I suppose I can understand the name given to hills.They would not have the same appeal as Norma Jean Baker's,which was her real name!"

His dining companion laughed. "I suppose not."

She leaned across and held out a hand.

"My name is Wendy, by the way. Wendy Griffiths"

Tom took her hand.

"Tom,Tom Stearsby. It's a pleasure to meet you."

He finished his meal and drained his cup.

"I think I will have another," he remarked. "Can I get you a cup?"

Wendy hesitated and then nodded.

"I really have to get going, but yes, please. Milk and one sugar, if you don't mind."

Tom returned with the coffees.

"Are you on the way home, then?" He enquired.

Wendy nodded.

"Yes, my husband will be waiting for me."

The thought came into Tom's mind- If only Mary was waiting at home for me, but he merely asked, "Do you live far?"

"I am on my way to Acklington. My husband is stationed at the RAF base there. I have been visiting a cousin who lives on a farm near Longhorsley. She had not seen Timothy since he was born. I stayed overnight but left early this morning because she had calving to see to. I decided I would stop here to give Timothy his bottle and change his nappy. Where are you headed?"

"Amble, I think. I need a change of clothing. I got quite wet last night and the stuff I have in my rucksack is all dirty. I hope there will be shops in Amble where I can buy new garments and perhaps a laundrette that can clean what I am wearing and the other stuff in the rucksack. I am not very presentable at the moment."

Wendy hesitated.

"I do not think you should consider doing any more hiking in your present state.Look,my car is outside.Why don't I give you a lift to Acklington where you can pick up a bus to Amble?"

Tom looked at her.Her cheeks were quite flushed.He considered it was due to her forwardness in making the offer.

"That is very kind of you,but I am a stranger to you.I could be a murderer on the loose for all you know!"

Wendy laughed.

"I think I am a good judge of character.My husband has taught me some means of self defence! I think I can handle you if you tried anything.You look quite tired anyway so I am not concerned. If necessary I will get Timothy to bite you.His first couple of teeth are showing through."

Tom grinned broadly.It was the first time since Mary died that he had a feeling of amusement."OK,fine.Thank you very much. I will accept your offer"

CHAPTER 25. FRIENDLY SUPPORT

In the car with the baby asleep and snuggled up safely on the back seat wrapped in a blanket,the two adults and chatted.Tom was able to take a closer look at his female companion.She was an attractive looking woman,dressed simply in a high necked plain woollen gown and wearing no cosmetic make up. He liked her clean honest look and her plain speaking. In many ways she reminded him of Mary. Concentrating on her driving, she appeared unaware of his attention.

Tom asked, "How long has your husband been in the Air Force?"

"About 6 years now, I think. I met him about three years ago when I was serving in the WAAF. He is a helicopter pilot with an Air Rescue unit. RAF Acklington is a gunnery training school for fighter pilots. They practice over the sea at target drones towed by other aircraft. It is quite an isolated area and there is no danger to civil aircraft. Warnings of practice days are sent out to civil aviation authorities and even shipping are asked to keep clear of the area. My husband is always on duty during the shooting practices in case of any accidents in the air. They rarely happen since safety precautions are always strictly observed but one never knows if an engine failure occurs and a pilot has to ditch in the sea. It is Jack's duty to rescue them. The main risk comes from flocks of birds flying into propellors or sucked into the jet engines.'"

"That sounds a worry," Tom commented. "Does that happen very often?"

"It is a rare occurrence but there is a large seabird colony on a reserve on Coquet island just off the coast. Puffins, terns, plovers, quillemots, kittywakes and fulmars."

"You know the names of all the species? Are you a bird lover?" Tom queried.

"Jack is.He grew up in Cresswell,which is a small village on Druridge Bay.It is popular to birdwatchers because there is a bird hide there.His parents lived nearby in a cottage.Jack spent all his time when not at school at the hide."

"So,do his parents still live there?"

"Sadly not.His father was a coal miner and worked in a pit near Morpeth.He was killed in an underground gas explosion about ten years ago."

"'Oh.What about his mother?"

"Gladys died of a broken heart about six months later."

Tom shook his head in sympathy.

"That's tough.What happened to the cottage?"

"Jack was their only child.He inherited it.Jack and I live in it now."

Tom looked surprised.

"I thought we were heading for Acklington?"

"We are.Jack has to be close at hand even when he is off duty so we have married quarters on the camp.We use the cottage when he is not flying and when he is on leave. Sometimes we rent it out for a week to holiday makers in the summer and bird watchers in the winter months.If you ever think of coming this way again on another hiking trip we would be pleased to have you stay."

Wendy opened the glove compartment and took out a pencil and notepad.

"Write down the address:

14 SANDCROFT RD. CRESSWELL. MORPETH NORTHUMBERLAND. NE61. TEL. NO. 01670 36542.

By the way, I have not asked you if you are married or not?"

Tom was startled by the question. His voice quavered slightly as he answered. "I was. My wife died in an accident. Are we near Acklington yet?"

Wendy glanced across at her passenger. It was plain that he did not want to expand on his answer.

"I am very sorry to hear that, Tom. Life can be cruel. Yes, the base is half a mile away. We will be there in less than ten minutes."

They sat in silence for the remainder of the journey. Wendy pulled up outside the airport's main entrance and put the car into neutral gear.

"Here we are, Tom. Sorry that I cannot take to all the way but the bus stop for Amble is just across the road. I hope you will get what you need in the town. If you decide to keep on hiking I suggest you visit Warkworth Castle which is short distance north of Amble. It has an interesting medieval history. Lindisfarne or Holy Island is also worth visiting if you want to go further north. Anyway, good luck. It was nice to meet you. Don't forget to give me a ring if you are ever in this area again."

A hand was held out for Tom to shake. He smiled back.

"It was nice to meet you, Wendy. Timothy too. Thanks for the lift."

He picked up his rucksack and climbed out. Wendy gave one last wave as she held out her identity card for perusal by the guard at the gate. Tim waved back and walked across the road to the bus stop. Half an hour later he was in Amble.

CHAPTER 26. COQUET ISLAND

Amble was a small coastal village which served both the fishing and the coal mining industry. Tom booked into the nearest hotel and paid for a week's accommodation in a single room It was mid-afternoon before he found a dry cleaner's retail store and deposited the wet and soiled clothing in his rucksack. In a men's outfitters he bought thermal underwear, long woollen socks and a waterproof jacket. He had a cup of coffee in a local cafe before he made his way down to the harbour and gazed at the fleet of fishing vessels tied up along the harbour wall. He remembered the small Merchant Navy button found in Mary's hand. Wainwright had obviously been a seaman at one time in his life and though he lived in the Tyneside area he may have had criminal connections in a small port like this. He was dead now, but what Tom wanted to know was how a petty criminal like Frankie Stevens became acquainted with him. If he could discover that and where Frankie may be hiding it may lead him to the stolen paintings from Peakview.He had to recover them and return them to Jenny to convince her that he was not involved in the robbery.Which led him to the next question.Who was the unidentified third party in that criminal deed? Could it have been an insider-someone who had been an employee at the grand manor?

Tom walked along the line of small fishing boats and wondered if he could make use of one to get across to Coquet Island.It was only three quarters of a mile offshore and apparently comprised fifteen acres in size, but it seemed ideal as a place of refuge. As a recognised bird reserve managed by the Royal Society for the Protection of Birds no authorised members of the public were allowed ashore, hence the human population consisted only of a few members of the Royal Society who managed the colony and cared for nesting birds during the summer months.In the winter the island was completely uninhabited except for the Lighthouse keepers who were in permanent residence. It did not seem too difficult to get ashore during hours of darkness if one avoided the lighthouse beam.

Gazing across at the island from the end of the long pier,Tom gave serious thought at attempting a landing.He was not by any stretch of the imagination an experienced mariner but he thought that he was capable of rowing or sailing across the short distance.It seemed to him that it was very possible that Frankie Stevens and his accomplices were somewhere on the island with the stolen paintings. He had to check it out.

In conversation with hotel staff and local residents over the next couple of days,Tom learned more about Coquet Island and the group of Farne Islands further north which lie between two and half and four miles off the Northumberland coast.They were close enough to make them worth Investigating.What further provoked his interest was the fact that Jennie's great uncle Sir William Johnstone had bought the group of islands in 1894 and also purchased the medieval castle at Bamburgh which dated back to Norman times.

Tom also learned the legendary story of local heroine, Grace Darling.Her brother and father,both named William, had been lighthouse keepers.William jnr.had been the very first Lighthouse keeper on Coquet Island.Father William was a lighthouse keeper on Longstone Island,one of the group of the Farne Islands.22 year old Grace lived with him.

In the early light of the morning of September 7th 1838 Grace saw from her bedroom window a paddle steamer anchored fast on rocks 600 yds below.It was the 400 ton two masted ss.Forfarshire,sailing from Hull to Dundee with 61 passengers aboard.It had lost all power to its engines and with only the use of its sails had been blown onto the rocks at 3 a.m.in a full gale.Its stern had been torn away and only the bow and fore section remained above water. Six of the crew managed to escape in a lifeboat leaving the surviving passengers clinging on to the wreckage in fear for their lives.

Grace urged her father to go their aid and they both set out in an open rowing boat which usually required propelling by three strong oarsmen.Rowing with all their strength,father and daughter reached the wreck to find only nine survivors who had not been swept away.One was a Mrs Dawson,who was clutching the drowned bodies of her two young children;a boy and a girl aged seven and five years old respectively.Grace comforted the mother while her father rowed the other passengers to safety.For their bravery William and Grace were given medals and publicly honoured.Sadly, Grace died four years later at the age of 26 from tuberculosis.

CHAPTER 27.NEW MANHUNT

In Amble's small public library Tom found a map of Coquet Island and checked the shoreline for accessible places to land. It was very rocky with few inlets where a boat could be safely beached.The fishing fleet along Amble harbour consisted of open,flat bottomed,high bowed boats of traditional Norman influence,suitable for landing on shallow sandy beaches.They were known as Cobles and could be dangerous if handled by an inexperienced crew.Grace Darling and her father used a coble in the rescue of passengers on the wrecked paddleship ss. Forfarshire.Tom wondered if he could handle such a vessel and considered an alternative.He had been a strong swimmer in his youth but had little opportunity to test his ability since becoming a farmer.Coquet Island was less than a mile away.Did he have the stamina to swim that far.In a calm sea possibly.In cold heavy Northumbrian waters,there had to be some doubt of survival.Nevertheless,if there was the possibility that Stevens was on the island with the Peakview Manor loot he had to investigate.He decided to think about it for a day or so.In the meantime he could check out Warkworth Castle.Wendy had suggested that Frankie could be hiding in that area.

Warkworth was serviced by the North Eastern railway line,so Tom caught a train there the next morning.The journey from Amble took less than 15 minutes.The original settlement of the village goes back to the 8th century but it only gained significance three centuries later with the building of the timber Motte and Baily castle on a mound overlooking the River Coquet.It withstood assaults by the Scots in the Anglo-Scottish wars but its defence was considered weak.The 1st Earl of Northumberland, head of the noble and powerful Percy family, remodelled It in brick and sandstone and added a Keep (a fortified tower) in 1370.

Tom found the castle in a ruined state but thought it was still imposing.More of interest to him was the 14th century hermitage built nearby onto and within a cliff face In the north bank of the River Conquet.Like all hermitages it provided a spiritual retreat for those who wished to be isolated from the world.If there was a place of refuge in Warkworth for Frankie Stevens and a hiding place for the stolen paintings it had to be here.The only access to it was by a ferry crossing half mile downstream from the castle.

On entrance, Tom discovered that the inner part of the

hermitage had two small chambers. One was a chapel with an altar and a tomb displaying the effigy of a female; the other room also had an altar but was otherwise empty. Tom searched around the Gothic architecture but there was no sign of any recent human occupation. He returned to the town feeling very disappointed. He had no option now except to risk the sea crossing to Coquet Island. A restless night was spent in a local inn followed by another fruitless search around the town before returning to Amble.

CHAPTER 28. DOUBTS

Tom awoke in the early hours of the next morning to the sound of rain beating against the window of his bedroom. It was blowing a gale outside. The weather conditions precluded any hope of reaching Coquet Island by boat and certainly put paid to any attempt at swimming across. He went down to breakfast in a sombre mood. With Wainwright and Longhurst both dead, was it worth more effort to search for his former cellmate? Tom had been lucky so far to have escaped detection but sooner or later he would be identified and returned to Pentonville to serve the remainder of his sentence. The police would eventually trace Stevens and the stolen artistry; he would receive a further stretch in prison for the theft and the pictures would be returned to Sir William's museum. What point was there in his continuation in searching for

Stevens? Since escaping from Pentonville his hunt for the two people responsible for Mary's death had been a complete failure. He had alienated Jenny and he could no longer rely on her friendship. She would not have disclosed to the Chief Constable that she knew Tom and given him assistance when he had arrived at her Rothbury farm: she would have been too embarrassed about that, but the fact remained that she no longer believed in his integrity. That disturbed Tom. The only highlight from the whole venture was his new acquaintanceship with Wendy.

Returning to his room after breakfast, Tom composed a letter to Sam explaining the current situation and indicated that he may soon return to Cornchester. He enquired about the farm and Benjie and asked Sam if he would put fresh flowers on Mary's grave. He addressed the letter c/o the Postmaster at Cornchester knowing that the police would check on all mail going to Wisteria Cottage. Sam went into the Post office at least once a week and Tom knew the Postmaster would hand the letter over to him. Though he did not condone Tom's killing of Longhurst he had great sympathy for him and would not betray him.

The rain had eased slightly as Tom walked to the nearest mailbox, though he noticed that heavy seas were still crashing against the harbour wall. Having posted the letter and collected his cleaned laundry he considered phoning Wendy but decided against it. He had nothing really to talk about and she may be busy with young Timothy. Her husband Jack would be in Acklington awaiting callouts. Flying a helicopter in this foul weather could be risky but it was when accidents at sea could happen and he was trained for the job.It occurred to Tom that he had not seen much aerial activity in the last couple of days,either military or civil aircraft.He had never flown and knew nothing about flight routes but he presumed that civil aircraft from Newcastle airport en route to Scotland and more northerly points would fly over the area.As for military aircraft,he had been told that the 7mile long Druridge Bay between Cresswell and Amble was used as an air gunnery practice range for the Royal Air Force with target drones being shot at by the new jet aircraft Gloster Meteor.There had been no sign of them either.

Tom walked down to Amble harbour the next morning with cleared skies overhead.He noted with relief that the sea had calmed.He hoped that he may be able to persuade one of the boat owners to take him out to have a closer look at Coquet Island.There were a number of Cobles missing from the quayside.The owners had obviously set out early to their fishing grounds In the hope of decent catches after missing out on the previous day.Tom spotted one fisherman dressed in oilskins preparing to sail.

He called out:

"I am interested in having a closer look at Coquet Island.I understand you are not allowed to land but would you be willing to take me close to the shoreline so that I can view the bird colony? I will pay you for the trouble."

The boat owner shook his head.

"Sorry, friend, but I have a whole day's fishing to catch up on. I can't spare the time. Perhaps another day."

Tom looked sympathetic.

"I understand, but I notice that you are alone. Do you usually go fishing on your own? It must be difficult to handle all your nets. I am not a fisherman but I would be glad to lend a hand."

The man looked doubtful.

"I am short of a man today. He is off sick but I cannot afford to lose another day. I may be able to use you. Can you swim? I don't want you falling overboard. Sharks are present in these waters."

Tom promised to be careful and would be responsible for his own safety.

"Come aboard, then. What's your name?"

"James," replied Tom.

"I'm Phiilip. There is a set of oilskins and a buoyancy jacket in the stern. A pair of rubber boots too. I don't want you slipping on the fish we catch. You will pay for any I cannot sell."

Tom nodded in acceptance and clambered aboard. He dressed quickly in the waterproofed clothing, feeling rather unsteady on his feet as he put on the leggings and boots. Philip's remarks about the presence of sharks in these waters were enough to dissuade him from the prospect of swimming to the island bird colony.

CHAPTER 29. THE ALBATROSS

In the next two hours Tom was kept busy as the boat sailed into deeper waters and Philip began heaving nets over the side. Twice he ignored the call,

"James, come and give me a hand here," before realising that he was the owner of the fictitious Christian name.

"Sorry, Philip." He pointed to the screeching seagulls overhead.

"They make such a racket I could not hear you."

"They are fishermen's constant companions, James, when they are out at sea. You will get used to them. Have you never heard the story of the Ancient Mariner?"

Tom shook his head.

"No? Actually it's a poem. Not all fishermen are illiterate, you know! It is about an old sailor who shoots an albatross with a crossbow. This large seabird was always a sign of good luck, so he was cursed for killing it. The albatross was hung round his neck as a sign of his guilt. From then onwards the crew of the ship he was aboard were cursed by bad luck. It's a long rhyme but well worth reading because now an albatross is a metaphor for a psychological burden that feels like a curse. It is where the couplet 'Water, water everywhere but not a drop to drink,' comes from."

Tom was startled by the story. Suddenly he felt that an albatross had been hung around his neck since he had lost Mary and the child she was carrying. His rage and hatred for those he blamed had led him to behave in ways he had never thought possible. This hunt for Frankie Stevens had to end! He decided not to go to Coquet Island after all. Let the police find his former cellmate. He would make his apologies to Jenny and hand himself in.

That night Tom had a very troubled dream. His mental stability had been questioned many times and psychiatric reports had helped in the reduction of his sentence for killing Longhurst. He knew he had acted irrationally since Mary's death but how disunited from reality had he become?

His nightmare suggested that he had assumed a split personality; that Frankie Stevens only existed in his own mind. It meant that Frankie was always with him even during his escape from Pentonville. Now he was connected to the robbery at Peakview. What about Wainwright? Was he also a figment of his troubled imagination? He had searched almost all of Northumberland and not found a trace of him. This was crazy! Wainwright had been sentenced with Longhurst even though he had not been present. Of course he was a real person, even in death at the grand mansion. Police records had identified him. As for Wendy and her six month old son, were they also part of his fantasies?

Tom woke up sweating profusely, his mind in turmoil. He searched his clothing and found the piece of paper with the address and phone number of Wendy's home at Cresswell. This was real! He would go there today and check it out.

CHAPTER 30. CRESSWELL

Tom dressed quickly and went down to breakfast.He checked the times of trains that ran through Amble to Newcastle.A stop at Widdrington meant a short bus journey to Cresswell.He decided not to ring Wendy and would arrive unannounced in case it was fictitious number and address.His nightmare was still fresh in his head.

The journey to Cresswell was uneventful and the village unremarkable:an ideal place for anyone who wanted to live in isolation.Tom was surprised that Wendy and her husband lived there but she had told him it had been inherited from his parents.He found Sandcroft Road, which comprised of no more than a dozen or so single storey dwellings. Most of them looked derelict and abandoned.This village was no holiday resort:Tom had learned that it was a place visited mainly by keen bird watchers as there was a bird colony nearby.Wendy had suggested that she rented her house on occasion to ornithologists.The beach was not suitable for holiday makers or sunbathers, since it was strewn with fossilised branches of trees and segments of washed up coal from the pits at Newbiggin-by-the-Sea which lay on the coast further south.Though the centre of the coal mining industry Newbiggin was a very popular holiday resort with a wide sandy beach,Cresswall was a far less desirable location.

14 Sandcroft Road was the second last cottage in the line of dwellings just off the beach.Tom approached the front entrance nervously.At least the property existed!He

hoped that it was inhabited;the detached property beside it certainly did not look as if it was.His knock on the door remained unanswered;he began to wonder if Wendy was at home.He was about to knock again when the door opened.Wendy stood there with a surprised smile on her face.

"Hullo,Tom.How nice to see you.Please come in."

She stood aside as he entered.In the gloom of the unlit interior he noticed the dark figure at the far end of the entrance hall. Tom wondered if it was Wendy's husband. He must be off duty.As he stepped forward into the room the other man advanced.

"Well,Tom,we were not expecting you yet,but we knew you would turn up sooner or later."

He came further into the light.Tom recoiled in horrified amazement as he recognised the figure.It was Frankie Stevens, holding a revolver in his hand.

"You have caught us by surprise,Tom.We thought you would still be at Warkworth or on Coquet Island looking for me!"

Tom,still reeling from the shock of seeing his former cell mate,finally found his voice.He turned to Wendy.

"What is happening here,Wendy?Has he been holding you hostage?"

She stepped forward so that she was standing beside Stevens.

"No, no,Tom.You are the hostage now.My name is not

JUST A SIMPLE COUNTRY BOY

Wendy, by the way. It's Pamela. Pamela Longhurst. I am the widow of the man you killed. I have been waiting a long time to get my revenge."

Tom was still gazing in amazement at her when he was knocked unconscious by a blow on the back of the head. When he regained his senses he found that he was bound tightly to a wooden kitchen chair in a room that looked like a cellar. The room was empty except for two large sacks made of rough hemp that were propped against the far wall at the end of the room.

CHAPTER 31. SUBTERFUGE

Pamela entered the dimly lit room an hour or so later and stood tight lipped in front of him. She was no longer the smiling humorous woman he had met at Granby Inn. She seemed to have read his mind.

"A different situation now, isn't it, Tom," she mocked.

"I knew it was you the moment you walked into the breakfast room at the Granby, but you also gave me your real name when you introduced yourself. I heard that you were a simple country boy and it is an accurate description, except for the killing of my husband. You swallowed my story hook, line and sinker, which is appropriate because it is what you will be doing very soon in a very painful way. Our first meeting was completely coincidental. I was on my way back to Acklington with Timmy-he is Pete's son, by the way. My cousin was looking after him while Frankie, Len Wainwright and I were in Peakview snatching Johnstone's art collection and other valuables. Poor Len fell off the cliff when we were getting away. That really shook me up!"

Tom could hardly believe what he was hearing.

"You took part in that robbery?"

"Oh, yes. It was planned months ago. Pete and I often did jobs together. All the Tyneside gang knew that Peakview was stuffed with valuable pieces of art. The problem was that so much of it is internationally recognisable. The disposal of it to dealers willing to take the chance of selling it on would have taken some time. I knew that after killing Pete you would want to track down Len in revenge for your wife's death. I did not know that you would come this far north but you had obviously heard that Len was a member of the Tyneside gang and decided to start your search in this area. I went into hiding as soon as our home address in Newcastle had been identified but I made a mistake in not taking his gun and the seaman's jacket with me. I joined him here in this cottage which has been a cover for us and other gang members for many years."

"But you dropped me off at Acklington and gave me this address! You told me where to go to look for Wainwright. I watched you drive into the airbase!"

"I know, Tom. I work part time in the Service canteen there. It helps to provide my cover. There is no husband Jack. I made him up. I know one or two helicopter pilots and ground crew but only through serving snacks and drinks.I told you to go to Warkworth and Coquet Island and look for Frankie and the stuff we took from the manor house because it gave us more time to sell off the artwork and valuables.It has been here all the time."

Pamela,alias Wendy,pointed to the heavy sacks in the opposite corner of the room.

"It is all in there."

Tom shook his head,

"I still do not understand!Why did you give me this address and telephone number?"

"Because I knew that you would contact me when you failed to find Frankie.I did not want you running around loose and discovering that there is no helicopter pilot named Jack Griffiths.I wanted you here to put an end to you for killing Pete. I expected you to ring me so that I would know the time of your arrival.It was a complete surprise when Frankie spotted you walking towards the cottage.We had estimated that we had a few more days before you came.You could not have spent long on the Island."

Tom tried to loosen his bonds by twisting his shoulders but the ropes did not yield.

"I did not go.I decided to return to London and hand myself in.Wainwright and your husband are no longer able to commit criminal offences.I don't hold too much of a grudge against Frankie except for his involvement in the robbery at Peakview.He is just a petty crook.The police will finally catch up with him.You too,and everything you have stolen will be recovered."

His female captor leaned forward and stared closely into his eyes.

"It's too bad that you interfered at all,Tom.You should have stayed on your farm.You would not be in this mess if you had.My husband would still be alive.I do not think that he deliberately shot your wife and killed your baby but these things happen if you are in the wrong place at the wrong time.My husband had already been convicted of robbery and manslaughter when you slashed his throat.I cannot forgive you for that and you will pay the price."

Tom felt the sting of a hard slap on his left cheek as she turned on her heel and walked away.The cellar door closed behind her.Her trussed up captive was left pondering his thoughts.They were not pleasant.

CHAPTER 32. EXPLANATIONS

Almost two hours passed by with Tom struggling to free himself from his bonds when Frankie Stevens walked in.

"You are wasting your time,Tom.Pete was an old sailor. He taught me how to tie knots."

He bent over and checked the ropes were still tight.

"I need to use the toilet, Frankie. Can't you untie me?" Tom implored in the hope that once free he could knock Stevens down and escape from the cellar.

"No, no, I can't do that! You will just have to pee in your pants. You will soon be wet all over when we take you for a boat ride."

Stevens grinned derisively.

"What do you intend to do with me?" Tom asked.

"Well, we will not leave you in the same way you left me outside Pentonville. That was not very nice of you, deserting your old cellmate. I had the devil of a job keeping up with you!"

Tom shook his head in puzzlement.

"Why would you want to? It astonished me to see you in Northumberland. You are an East End Londoner. You could not have known Longhurst or Wainwright!"

"Ah, but I did! Wainwright, anyway. He had been in and out of prison almost as many times as I have. I met him in Wandsworth when I was doing a stretch for burglary. We got together after finishing our sentences and did a few robbery jobs. He brought me up to Gateshead one time and I met a few of the Tyneside gang. Including Peter Longhurst and his wife."

"But why would you want to follow me after our escape?"

"Tom, you forget that you talked in your sleep. I was in the bottom bunk, remember. I heard you mumble about going after Wainwright if you got out because you blamed him for killing your wife. You had already killed Longhurst. Len had become a mate of mine so I had to do what I could to stop you doing that. After you left me in the street I knocked an old man down who was exercising his dog. I was glad that it was only a poodle and not a bull terrier! Anyway, I stripped him, put on his clothes, found few pounds in the pockets and tried to catch up with you. Although I didn't know where you were going I took a guess and hitched a few lifts from lorry drivers going north. Finally I got to Newcastle, contacted a couple of blokes who were members of the Tyneside gang. They gave me Pam's address. The rest you know. We broke into Peakview and robbed the place. It was well known that Johnstone was a very wealthy man. After that, Pamela told me that she had met you accidentally at the pub in Framlington. Although you did not tell her you were hunting for Len we guessed you were, and in finding him you would have found us too. In fact, because you knew Johnstone's great niece, you had heard about the robbery and that Len and I were involved. Your interest then became finding the loot and getting it returned. Well, Tom, you have heard the expression that curiosity killed the cat. Today, or rather later tonight, it will kill you."

Alone once more in the cellar, Tom reflected on the information Frankie had given him. He had always wondered how his former cell mate had been connected with the two robbers from Tyneside. It was a simple explanation. As for his own present predicament he had no doubt what was now planned for him.He needed to escape in a hurry. Desperation forced him to have another attempt to free himself.With all the strength that he could muster he began to rock the chair from side to side until it toppled over.It hid the floor hard.Tom lay still for a moment listening for any movement from the room above. Silence.He breathed a sigh of relief.The ropes binding his lower limbs to the legs to the chair seemed to have slightly loosened.They loosened more as he tried to kick out with his feet.His arms and hands were still tightly bound to the rails at the back of the chair.From his awkward position he twisted his neck around.There was nothing in the room that could help him extricate himself.Except perhaps in the sacks leant on the far wall? It was worth checking. Using his body strength,he managed to swivel the chair so that he faced the hemp sacks;he gripped the floor with the backs of his ankles and tried to propel himself forward.Inch by inch the chair moved in the direction of the wall,scraping the floorboards as it did so.Tom stopped and listened after every squeak and scrape.Still no indication that the clatter and scraping had been heard in the rooms above. Encouraged,he strained every sinew in sliding the chair forward.Finally he reached the sacks and could see the protruding corners of the varnished frame that held one of the artistic masterpieces stolen from Sir William's mansion.

With his hands tied behind his back and lying sideways on the floor,Tom was unable to see the contents of the sacks,but he knew that Jenny's great uncle had a collection of weaponry in his museum that would be extremely valuable.Using his feet,Tom tipped over both sacks so that they lay beside him.The large paintings remained inside the thick burlap but Tom had no interest in them at that moment. Scattered around his feet were gold goblets,a Derringer pistol,an Apache revolver,which consisted of a pistol and knife combined,a short cutlass and many other pieces of antique armament.Tom was studying all of these artefacts and wondering how he could pick up the cutlass and use it to sever his bonds when he heard footsteps behind him.From his viewpoint he could only see trousered legs.Craning his neck,he looked up at Frankie's face.

CHAPTER 33. ABORTED ESCAPE ATTEMPT

"You keep surprising me,Tom!I see you have found our cache.We had hoped to have disposed of that before you got here."

Frankie leaned down and uprighted the chair.

"I will give you credit,Tom.It must have taken some effort to get over to here.I never heard a thing.I came down just to check on the ropes.Pamela has taken Timmy to a friend to be minded while she and I end your interference. You have been a damned nuisance,though you did help me get out of Pentonville.It's bad enough having the Old Bill chasing me without you joining the hunt.I will always be looking over my shoulder while you are still breathing."

Tom felt himself dragged back to the centre of the room.He watched while Stevens replaced the stolen items into the sacks.

"I hope you have not scratched the canvases,Tom. Pam will not be very pleased.I do not know much about art but I have been told that they are worth hundreds of thousands,if not millions of pounds.Selling them on or even returning them for a ransom will keep me very comfortable in my old age."

Frankie checked that Tom's arms were still tightly bound behind the chair.

"I will leave your legs loose because you are going to have to walk to the harbour as soon as it gets dusk.Now please be sensible and behave.Pam will not hesitate to give you a good beating if you don't."

Tom let out a curse as Stevens walked back up the stairs.It annoyed him that he had been led into a trap. Longhurst's wife's story had been so convincing that not only had he believed her but had been attracted by her easy charm.He would not be so naïve and trusting in the future.Not that there was a future if she and Stevens were successful in their deadly scheme of disposing of him. Dying did not unduly bother him now that Mary and their unborn child would be absent from his life.The two men responsible for that tragic loss were both dead and even if he stayed alive he would still spend many years in prison serving the rest of his sentence.Sam would probably move into Wisteria Cottage and maintain the farm and care for the livestock.What concerned him most was that he would die with Jenny believing that he was an unscrupulous liar and a thief.

Two hours later Frankie and Pamela came down to the cellar dressed in waterproof oilskins.Tom was almost pleased to see them.His arms and hands had lost any feeling and his neck and shoulders ached.It was a relief to be free from the chair and stand up straight.

Neither of his captors spoke as they marched him up the stairs to the front entrance to the house.Dusk was falling as the front door was locked.Tom's two escorts placed themselves either side of him.Each took a firm grip of an elbow and turned him towards the harbour.A light mist was forming as they walked slowly towards the lines of Cobles.There was not a soul to be seen.Shouting for help would not get any reaction.Tom thought of breaking free and running back to the centre of the village but he was stiff from sitting in the kitchen chair for hours.He knew he would not get very far before he was caught.He turned his head towards Frankie and defiantly muttered,

"You will not get away with this.Somebody will see us."

"It does not matter if they do.We are just three people going night fishing.Many do,though usually on a better evening than this.Anyway don't try anything because there is a gun in your back.It is fitted with a silencer and I will shoot you if I have to.I would rather not because a boating accident is planned for you.Now, just keep walking right to the end of the harbour wall."

Having reached the end of the fishing boats tied up against the harbour wall, Frankie gestured Tom to stop and pointed at a small blue painted Coble.

"In you get, Tom. Sit on the gunwhale for a moment."

Tom did as he was bid. In the bottom of the boat was a heap of fishing nets with lead weights attached. He suspected that they were not there for their usual purpose. Frankie noticed Tom's glance.

"Yes, my friend. They are to ensure that you don't come up to the surface and embarrass us."

He grinned at Pamela as she sat down at the stern. She remained stony faced and did not reply. Tom began to rise to his feet. Stevens waved the gun.

"No, no! Don't be alarmed. I will make sure you are fast asleep when you go under. You won't feel a thing! But first you have some work to do. You are going to help me to row to the middle of the bay where the water is deepest."

Another wave of the revolver emphasised his order.

"Now move to the seat in front of me and pick up that oar."

Tom had no choice but to obey. Slowly the small fishing boat moved away from the harbour wall and entered the open bay. The water became choppy and the mist became thicker, reducing visibility. The murky conditions added to Tom's puzzlement. Why have his captors gone to all this trouble to kill him when they could have done so in the cottage? He reasoned that they did not want the trouble of disposing of his body or being connected with his disappearance.He had left some of his belongings in his room at the hotel in Amble and conversed with the staff about going to Cresswell and Coque Island.Moreover,he had not settled a final bill because he had expected to return.That fact alone would mean that the hotel owner was likely to contact the police, who would then make their own enquiries.Possibly they may discover that Tom had been on a fishing trip with Philip and had talked about visiting Coquet Island.The police may even knock door to door at the few habitable houses near Cresswell harbour,which meant that Stevens was at risk of being caught.His description had been circulated to the local constabulary because of his involvement in the Peakview robbery.Those concerns about police investigations may have led Longhurst's widow to the conclusion that the best way to dispose of Tom was to dump him in the sea where he could never be found.Could he have been killed in the cottage?Yes,but he was needed alive to help row the boat to the centre of the lake.Stevens was no expert oarsman and Pamela needed to conserve her strength for the return journey back to the harbour.

CHAPTER 34. DANGEROUS WATERS

As the darkness set in around the boat and the sea became blacker, Pamela produced a torch and shone it on Tom's back.

"Keep rowing, Tom. Another fifteen minutes we should be in the centre of the bay. You can stop then and even say a prayer. That is more than you gave Pete before you slashed his throat."

"And more time Mary had before he shot her and the baby," retorted Tom, with bitterness in every tone.

"He got what he deserved."

Her reply was a sharp smack on the back of his skull. The impact broke the torch bulb and the boat was plunged in darkness. At that very moment there was a loud blast from a ship's siren. Looming up behind them was a large cruiser ship. A very bright light illuminated the coble from stem to stern. As the bow of the passenger liner towered over the small fishing boat a megaphoned voice boomed out. "You are in the main shipping lane! Move over or else you will be swamped."

The warning came almost too late. The fishing boat rocked wildly as the liner slid by. A huge wave lifted the flat-bottomed coble into the air where it hovered momentarily before crashing back down again. The three drenched occupants landed heavily on the deck. Pamela had hit her head on the side of the gunwhale and was lying unconscious. Tom seized his chance. He picked up one of the fallen oars and thrust the blade into the middle of Frankie's chest.Stevens let out one startled cry as he stumbled backwards and disappeared into the raging sea.Another wave from the departing liner swept him further away from the fishing boat that was now half filled with water.Tom briefly caught sight of him gesticulating wildly with upraised arms.Whatever words or screams he emitted went unheard.Before darkness descended again Tom thought he saw the top of a shark's fin moving in the direction of his former cell mate.

Pamela Longhurst was still lying unconscious at the back of the boat.Tom checked her over.Her forehead was badly gashed and one of her legs were twisted awkwardly at the knee.He tried to move her into a more comfortable position but he did not want to aggravate any other injury she may have sustained.He was angered by her villainous and dishonest behaviour but he reminded himself that she had a young son who was dependent on her.He was not responsible for the criminal acts of his parents.His own son would have been distraught at losing his mother.

Tom looked around for means of baling out the boat,which was lying heavily on the turbulent waves.He found a wooden tray which was normally used to hold the fish caught in the nets.Slowly he emptied the sea water over the side until the boat was navigational.In the darkness he was uncertain of the direction of the shore line but he calculated that it would be on his port side. He turned the coble and steered in that direction.There was no moon to guide him but after twenty minutes of rowing he sighted the Cresswell harbour lights shining dimly ahead on the starboard side. He renewed his efforts, struggling with the oars and straining arms and shoulders to advance the sluggish movement of the small vessel. Pamela had begun to moan and twist her head around. Tom knew he had to get medical attention for her as quick as he could. Thank God that the boat had stayed afloat. He had been a strong swimmer in his youth but there was no way he could have kept the injured female's head above water for the length of time it would have taken to swim to the shore.

CHAPTER 35. BACK TO DRY LAND

Tom berthed the Coble against the harbour wall as gently as he could. Pamela's head movements indicated that she was gradually regaining her senses, but she was in no physical state to go anywhere without help. Tom left her on the bench seat and walked quickly to the harbourmaster's office. It was closed but there was a public telephone box beside it. Tom dialled the emergency number and asked for an ambulance before returning to the boat. Pamela had opened her eyes but still looked dazed. Tom waited until the ambulance arrived and two medics carried her to the emergency vehicle. He gave a false name and address for himself and his injured companion; asked the location of the hospital she would be taken to, and stated he would ring the following day to learn of her condition. He watched the ambulance drive away before walking back to Sandcroft Road. It was still the early hours of the morning with mist still in the air when he broke a window and entered No.14.

Tom went directly down to the cellar and checked the contents of the two large hemp sacks.He was pleased to see that the artwork looked undamaged.One was a Lowry;another was signed by Van Gogh.He knew Jenny would be delighted to hear the news that all the stolen items from Peakview had been recovered and were in good order.He thought about ringing her direct but he was hesitant to do so,remembering how angry she was with him during their last telephone conversation.He decided that he would contact the police in the first instance and give them the address where the stolen masterpieces could be found. He smelled a combination of perspiration and sea salt on his body.A bath and a stiff drink were the first priorities.

An hour later,refreshed in body and mind,Tom picked up the phone and rang the local police.He explained to the astonished desk sergeant that all the items taken during the burglary at Peakview Manor could be found at an address in Sandcroft Road,Cresswell.There was nobody at home so forceful entry would be required.He put the telephone down when he was asked to identify himself. Despite the anonymous call he knew that the given information would be checked.He searched around the cottage to ensure that nothing had been left that would incriminate him before walking out and catching the public transport back to Amble. At the hotel he rang the local hospital at Cresswell and enquired about a female patient named Wendy Griffiths.

"Oh, yes," the receptionist responded.

"This is the lady brought in by ambulance from Cresswell harbour, is that correct? Are you the gentleman that called us?"

Tom nodded before realising that the girl at the other end could not see him.

"'Yes, that is correct."

"Just one moment, sir. What is your name?"

"Tim Cranby," said Tom. hoping that the patient would get the connection and know it was him.

The answer came back a few minutes later.

"Mrs Griffiths is doing quite well, sir, though she has no memory of arriving back at the harbour. Her head wound has been stitched and a plaster cast has been applied to the left fibula. She will be hopping around for a couple of days but it is expected that she will be discharged after that and put in the care of her local doctor."

"That's good," commented Tom and rang off.

His next call was to Sam's home telephone. His wife Barbara answered.

"Oh, Tom. It is so good to hear from you. Where are

you?Sam has been really worried about you.He is up at the farm now,waiting for cattle feed deliveries."

"I cannot tell you where I am,Barbara,but tell Sam I am coming back to London tomorrow.I will meet him at the cottage sometime in late afternoon."

Tom closed the call after Barbara expressed her pleasure at the news.He did not want to answer any questions that she may have asked.It was possible that Sam's home number was being tapped and though he intended to hand himself in at Cornchester police station he did not want to be arrested before he tied up all the loose ends.He packed his few belongings in the rucksack Jenny had provided and went downstairs to pay the hotel bill.He had decided to spend his last day in Northumberland at Morpeth where he and Mary had spent part of their honeymoon.From Morpeth he could catch a train direct to King's Cross railway station.

CHAPTER 36. RELIVING HAPPY MEMORIES

It took less than one and half hours to reach the historic market town of Morpeth,which lies on the bank of the River Wansbeck and just a few miles from the coastal resort of Newbiggin -by- the -Sea.Tom booked into a small hotel for a one night stay and took a relaxed stroll around the town.He wanted to enjoy his last hours of freedom before he was penned up again in a prison cell.Mary and he had enjoyed a wonderful honeymoon at this rural location and sunbathed on the long sandy beach at the the nearby seaside resort. He had captured many magical moments in his mind but what had delighted them most was on that wondrous day a few months later when Mary had discovered she was pregnant. The joy of that moment had been indescribable. And yet the ecstasy had turned to horror on the day of the post office robbery. With his world blown apart it was no wonder that he had sought vengeance on the two perpetrators and had attempted to follow a trail which would lead to their destruction.

It was ironic that the beginning and end of the tragedy would end here in Morpeth because Tom had discovered the town's name was derived from a 17th century word Morthpaeth, which means Murder Path, in remembrance of some forgotten slaying in the road leading to the old village. The village was recorded in the Northumberland Assizes Rolls of 1256 as Morepath. History had repeated itself.

Tom took a bus into Newbiggin and strolled along the promenade, remembering the days spent romping and laughing with Mary during their honeymoon. He had loved her with all his heart and found it difficult to believe that she was willing to share his simple farming life. He soon discovered that she loved animals and was in her element helping with the cattle and sheep: even mucking out was never an irksome duty. He closed his eyes and wished that he could hold her and their son in his arms

The next morning Tom took the North-Eastern train

line back to London.The black hair dye no longer hid his blonde locks:he had discarded his false spectacles somewhere in Cresswell.A disguise was no longer needed.

Within two hours after arriving at King's Cross he was walking up the garden path of Wisteria Cottage.The door opened before he reached it and Benjie bounded out with tail wagging furiously. Sam stood smiling on the threshold.

"Come in,Tom.It's good to see you.Barbara told me that you would be coming home today."

Tom looked around.Nothing had changed except Mary was not there to welcome him with a kiss.

"Let me relieve you of that rucksack,Tom.You look rather knocked out.Have a seat and I will make a drink."

The exhausted traveller dropped gratefully into his favourite chair.Benjie came towards him and nuzzled his face between his knees.His tail wagged even harder as Tom stroked and patted his head.

Over the next two hours the two men chatted almost nonstop.Tom told his farm hand all the events that had occurred since his escape from Pentonville.Sam listened with some astonishment before relating what had occurred on the farm since he had taken over.The police had called a few times and had checked all the outbuildings.The local postmaster had been questioned and Sam's home had been searched after Tom's escape but no members of the local or national police force had been seen in the area since then.It was expected that all incoming calls to Wisteria Cottage would be recorded but it was not known if Sam's home telephone number was being tapped. Since no police had turned up at the cottage after Tom's call to Barbara it was presumed that it had not been heard.

After Sam had gone home, Tom felt too tired to do much else than wrap a blanket around himself and lie back in the armchair. He could not face the prospect of sleeping in the double bed upstairs: he went off to sleep very quickly and it was daylight before he awoke. He made a strong cup of black coffee and took it up to his shower room. Fortunately the electric boiler was still operative. He disrobed and threw all the discarded garments into a corner. Standing under the shower unit, he allowed the gush of hot water to cascade all over his body, removing the last remaining traces of the hair dye and the fetid smell of stale sweat. He had showered every day after working in the fields tending the livestock but never had he felt so thankful for the invigorating downpour that immersed him. He shaved and dressed in clean clothes and looked at himself in the mirror. His image stared back at him. He had lost weight and the strain etched on his face from the horror of the years since losing Mary was clear to see, but he looked presentable. He still faced the prospect of several more years in gaol but his mission to see the end of the two criminals responsible for his mental anguish had been accomplished.

Sam called while Tom was having breakfast. He rejected the offer of coffee and asked what plans Tom had.

"First, I am going to walk around the farm and look at the animals. Sam, I know you have done a brilliant job of caring for them and you will continue to have that duty in the future if you are happy to carry on. I am going to hand myself in the police station later on as I promised Jenny that I would do. How long a sentence I will get for escaping I do not know, but I expect I will have to serve the rest of the original time I was given for killing Longhurst. I suggest that it would be more convenient for you and Barbara to move into here with your two children, but that is up to you. I shall leave it and the farm to you in my will anyway. I have no other close relatives that are more entitled to it than you."

Sam murmured his thanks. Tom waved them away.

"I could not have kept the farm going without your help, Sam. I will always be grateful to you. Now, let's go and look at the livestock. I am anxious to see them. They have been in the fields all night."

Tom toured all around the farm for the rest of the morning and satisfied himself on the condition of the sheep and cattle. He remarked on the number of new lambs and calves that had been born during his absence.

"They all look very healthy, Sam. You may need to get a couple more barns built to accommodate them when the weather is bad. I suggest that you take on a couple more farmhands to help you out. I will let you get on now, as I have a couple of letters to write before I leave."

Tom returned to the cottage and wrote out a cheque for £800 payable to Jenny. An accompanying letter expressed his regret at his deceit and he thanked her for not exposing him to the Chief Constable.He added the hope that the Peakview artwork and other stolen items had been found and returned safely to the Johnstone mansion.He confirmed that he would be handing himself to the police as she had advised.Tom sealed the envelope and went to find Sam He found him in the milking shed.

"I am leaving now,Sam.I am going to have a word with the Postmaster before handing myself in at the police station.There is no point in delaying now.I will be in touch as soon as I know where I will be going.You have my authorisation to handle all the bills that come in.I expect you have been taking your wages from the payments received from the dairy income and that is fine. Buy whatever you need to keep the farm maintained, including the building of those extra barns.I trust you completely,Sam."

He shook hands with his dependable aide,who had become a staunch ally.Benjie was at his heel,waiting for instructions.Tom went down on his knees and ruffled the terrier's head.

''You have been a loyal companion,too,old friend.I shall miss you,but Sam is your master now.I know you like him and you work well together in the fields.Stay with him now."

Benjie looked puzzled but stood beside Sam as Tom walked away.He had formed a bond with the farm hand in Tom's absence.His former master was pleased about that.

Tom posted the letter to Jenny and went to have a

chat with the postmaster,who was very surprised by his appearance.Tom thanked him for his friendship and enquired about his health;he was assured that the injuries sustained during the assault by Wainwright and Longhurst had healed.Tom informed him that the two attackers had died and justice had been served.The Postmaster expressed some satisfaction for that although he already knew that Tom had been convicted of killing Longhurst. Tom then gave him a brief resume of the events that had taken place since his prison escape with Frankie Stevens,omitting details of the demise of his former cell mate.He concluded by stating that he had returned home to Cornchester to give himself in to the local police.

Tom took the short walk to the police station,struggling with some nervousness.Once inside the premises he straightened his shoulders and addressed the desk sergeant.

"My name is Tom Stearsby.I believe you have been looking for me?"

The police officer looked up from the files he was studying.

"Sorry,say that again?"

Tom repeated.

"I am Tom Stearsby.I escaped from Pentonville a couple of months ago.I believe police forces have been searching for me."

The sergeant stared at him open mouthed before grabbing a telephone.Within minutes Tom was surrounded by uniformed officers and his arms pinioned behind him. He protested.

"Take it easy! I have just given myself in. I am not going anywhere!"

His protest remained unanswered. Two officers patted him down and searched for weapons. Behind the desk all hell had broken loose. The desk sergeant was making telephone calls one after another. Police records were being studied. Tom stood quietly against a wall, amazed at all the uproar his simple statement had generated. Ten minutes later his identity was confirmed and he was pushed into a holding cell. Two hours passed by. Reluctantly he was given a cup of tea that he had requested. Finally the cell door opened and two CID men dressed in civilian clothing took him to an interview room. An unknown female solicitor accompanied them. Tom identified himself again, confirmed his age and home address and that he was an escapee from Pentonville Prison. To every other question, including the location of his former cell mate and fellow escapee Frankie Stevens, he answered, "No comment."

Eventually he was taken back to his cell.

CHAPTER 37. REFLECTIONS

Three days later Tom found himself in solitary confinement in the D Wing of HMP Wormwood Scrubs, West London. The Scrubs, as it was familiarly known, was a High Security prison. D wing was used for those prisons considered high risk potential escapers. Tom was due to be contained there until the Crown Prosecution Service had considered his case and decided on the extension of his sentence due to his breakout from Pentonville.

Tom did not mind being in solitary confinement. It gave him time to think. Three years before he had been just a country boy with a lovely wife, a child on the way and a happy life ahead with everything he could have ever hoped for. He could never have imagined that he would become a double killer and end up in prison. One callous act by two thieves had destroyed all his dreams and taken away the woman he loved and the son he had longed for. No wonder that the grief of their loss had affected his mental state to the degree that all he could think about was gaining revenge on the perpetrator. He felt no guilt in killing Longhurst or for wanting to hunt down Wainwright. Frankie Stevens' death was a simple matter of self defence. Kill or be killed. With regard to Pamela Longhurst, he realised that she had acted in the same way that he did when hearing about Mary's killing. She was also consumed by hate and rage and determined to avenge her husband's death. They shared the same emotions in losing the person they loved. Tom remembered the loving care she took of her young son Timothy in the Granby hotel and accepted that she was a devoted mother. She had in fact reminded him of Mary and he had been disappointed by her duplicity. He wondered what sort of a girl she had been before meeting up with Longhurst? Had he charmed her into helping him with his criminal activities? Tom had learned that many young women were attracted to rogues like Longhurst because they were exciting to be with: in contrast to other nicer, more decent men who were often dull lovers.

Tom wondered if Pamela had left hospital and been reunited with her son. If the police had found the two sacks in her cellar, she would have some awkward questions to answer.

Ten days later Tom received a letter from Jenny. Her colleague the Chief constable had informed her that the escapee named Stearsby had handed himself in and been sent to Wormwood Scrubs. Jenny thanked Tom for his cheque but said it was unnecessary, since he had traced her great uncle's possessions and notified the police of the address where they could be found. Wendy Griffiths had been identified as the wife of Peter Longhurst and she had admitted her part in the robbery. No mention was made of the other thief, Frankie Stevens. Jenny realised that Tom had no part in the Peakview theft and apologised for doubting his honesty. She regretted that she could do nothing about any increase in Tom's sentence, but she would recommend an early parole. Further than that, knowing that Tom had bequeathed Wisteria Farm to

Sam, she would find another plot of agricultural land with an attached cottage and restock the new farm with cattle and sheep from her own breeds.

Tom was thrilled by the news. He would deal with the increased jail sentence when it came. As for Mrs. Longhurst, she was awaiting trial. Her young son would be taken into care and possibly put up for adoption. Tom reflected on that. Perhaps if he and Pamela were released about the same time and she had changed her ways and regretted her past criminal life, they may meet up again. She would know that Tom had saved her life when he could have thrown her overboard and allowed her to drown. Would she think of him in a different light? Could he forgive her for aiding and abetting her husband's criminality? Could they reach a new understanding and form a relationship? Was there any hope for a brighter future ahead for either of them after they had been released? In Tom's case, yes, if Jenny's promises came to fruition, but would he be happy living alone? As for Pamela Longhurst, would she be able to reclaim her young son on her release? What would she do then?

Tom remembered that Pamela, alias Wendy, had named all the species of birds on Coquet Island. Perhaps in her youth she had been a more caring, gentle girl with respect and compassion for all animals. Would she find happiness in changing her lifestyle and settling down on a farm? Would her teenage son Timmy enjoy working with animals? Who knows? Lots of unanswered questions for the future, but you cannot live in the past forever. Tom would always love

Mary and regret the loss of their unborn son but strange and unexpected things do happen. He did not know all the answers, but after all, he was just a simple country boy.

END

CPSIA information can be obtained
at www.ICGtesting.com
Printed in the USA
BVHW062258011221
622919BV00005B/26

9 781665 537230